With a SILENT COMPANION

FLORIDA ANN TOWN

NORTHERN LIGHTS YOUNG NOVELS

Red Deer Press

Northern Young Novels are published by
Red Deer Press
56 Avenue & 32 Street Box 5005
Red Deer Alberta Canada T4N 5H5

Credits
Edited for the Press by Peter Carver
Cover art by Igor Kordey
Cover design by Duncan Campbell
Text design by Amy Becker
Printed and bound in Canada by Friesens for Red Deer Press

Acknowledgments
Financial support provided by the Canada Council, the Department
of Canadian Heritage and the Alberta Foundation for the Arts, a
beneficiary of the Lottery Fund of the Government of Alberta.

THE CANADA COUNCIL | LE CONSEIL DES ARTS
FOR THE ARTS | DU CANADA
SINCE 1957 | DEPUIS 1957

Canadian Cataloguing in Publication Data
Town, Florida.
With a silent companion
(Northern lights young novels)
ISBN 0-88995-211-6
1. Bulkley, Margaret Anne—Juvenile fiction. I. Title. II. Series.
PS8589.O957W5   1999   jC813'.54   C99-910347-4
PZ7.T69Wi 1999

5 4 3 2 1

Contents

Author's Acknowledgments

Special thanks must go to a number of people who contributed to this project in many ways. To Fred Bodnaruk, whose comment provided the initial spark; to Tex Thorpe, who gave so generously of his skill; to the patient librarians at Port Coquitlam's Terry Fox Library, who ordered obscure books at my request and must have wondered at my strange taste in literature; to Joe Currie of the Edinburgh University Library; to Dr. M. Devine of the Horace Walpole Library in Connecticut; to Roanne Mokhtar, a reference archivist in the National Archives of Canada; to librarians in the public library in Cork who patiently guided me through their stacks; to librarians in Cape Town, South Africa, who searched their records for me; to the Royal Art Society in Britain; Maritime Museums in many locations; to Jill Leach at the office of the British High Commissioner; to editors who published my pleas for information throughout nations that were once part of the British Commonwealth and figured in Dr. Barry's story; to Allan Shute for encouragement; to Pearl Novotny of the University of Manitoba's Alumni Association; to attendants in the Reading Room of Ireland's National Archives; to Daniel Glenney of the Canadian War Museum; to librarians at the Ministry of Defence, Middlesex, England; to the British Defence Liaison Staff at the British High Commission in Ottawa; to Miss L.J. Pringle of the Naval Pay and Pensions Accounts office in Hants, England; to Mrs. Y.H. Kennedy of the Historical Records Office Royal Marines, also in Hants; to Christine Weideman, Archivist at Yale University; to Liza Verity of the National Maritime Museum, London; to Martina Aherne of the Diocese of Cloyne in Mallow, County Cork; to Sister M. Angela Bolster of the Cork–Ross Diocesan Archives; to Antonia Moon of the India Office Records of the British Library, London; to William B. Bidwell of Yale University; to Robie Almes, head of reader services department at the Public Record Office in Kew, England; to Susan Bethune and to Heiki Johrden of Port Moody.

Kim Town Schon and Tia Town-Schon deserve thanks as

well. They listened all the way to Disneyland and provided input that was both interesting and useful. To anyone who has inadvertently been omitted, my apologies.

Special thanks must go to my editor, Peter Carver, whose sensitive and generous comments have been most helpful and who gave this story a second chance.

Most of all I thank my husband, Hugh, for allowing James Barry to become a member of our family during the years that I chased this will-o'-the-wisp through faded documents in locations around the world. His patience and encouragement were endless and kept my enthusiasm high.

To Hugh, as always,
and to Kathy and Stewart, Stuart and Lyn,
Ian and Jennie, and to Nick, Joey, Max,
Tori, Britti, Alex, AJ, Christopher and Nathanial,
and especially to Kim and Tia,
who listened all the way to California.

The search for Dr. James Barry began by accident. My original intent was to write the life story of another doctor, Dr. Claire Magdelene Onhauser Seale, better known to me as Aunt Madge. Madge was one of my mother's three older sisters and one of only half a dozen women enrolled in medicine at the University of Manitoba. In the 1920s female doctors were uncommon.

During the course of my research into the career of my aunt and some of Canada's first female doctors, there were puzzling references to a female doctor who had been practising even earlier than the traditionally acknowledged first group. In several accounts there was a disclaimer to the effect that "except for Dr. James Barry," Emily Stowe and Jennifer Trout were the first female doctors in Canada. But who was Dr. Barry? Why was a military surgeon included in the discussion? How did Dr. Barry fit into the picture? And why was he—or she—an exception? My original objective was put aside. First I had to learn more about the mysterious Dr. Barry.

Chapter One

CORK

WHEN MARGARET ANNE BULKLEY was born more than two hundred years ago in the bustling Irish seaport of Cork, no one suspected she would one day become the centre of one of the greatest mysteries in medical history. Her childhood was very ordinary. Her working-class parents were Mary Anne Barry and Jeremiah Bulkley. Her maternal grandparents were Juliana Reardon and John Barry. They lived nearby in Blackpool, a residential area in Cork where stone-built houses clustered together in tight groups on the rolling hillsides along the northern bank of the River Lee.

The Lee was the lifeblood of the city, alive with small boats that ferried goods and passengers across the river from one point to another. A series of low bridges spanned the Lee, stitching together the flat plain, where business and commercial shops were located, and the numerous residential subdivisions on the hillsides. The surrounding countryside was green and rolling, dotted with flocks of sheep and, here and there, a herd of cows.

These were the only scenes familiar to Margaret as a child. Each day on her way to school, she walked down St. Patrick Street, from the Blackpool area in the hills behind town, across the bridge spanning the busy river. She loved to watch the tugs and boats bustling back and forth from one quay to the next, stopping to load and unload goods and passengers. She imagined trade goods and people coming from exotic places, whose names she couldn't pronounce.

On her way home from classes, Margaret liked to walk along Carey's Lane, where there was a small Catholic chapel. Almost every Sunday at confession, Margaret had to tell the priest that, once again, she had lost her temper. Usually it was over something that wasn't even important. And it didn't seem to matter how many Hail Marys or Our Fathers she said, the next week she'd have to report she'd done it again. Margaret's temper was her biggest problem. She wished she could be more like her mother, who never seemed to get angry or upset.

During the week, though, Margaret passed the chapel and continued directly home. Sometimes, though, she couldn't resist stopping for just a moment to watch the activity around the new Butter Exchange building. Her father said merchants were getting rich there selling good Irish salted butter to Britain, Europe and the West Indies. She liked to imagine her uncles sitting somewhere in the West Indies, eating butter from Cork and perhaps remembering the family left at home.

Walking over the North Gate Bridge, Margaret could see the pepper-pot top of Shandon Steeple on the next hill over from Blackpool. There was a Protestant Church of Ireland, the country's official church, on the broad avenue running parallel to the river. Margaret walked past it on her way home although she stayed on the far side of the road. Even though the church wasn't Catholic, its bells still sounded lovely. Sometimes the bells of the different churches sounded as though they were talking together, their different voices blending in a wordless song.

Once past the church, Margaret walked more quickly, lest she be accused of dawdling on the way home. As the only daughter she had many chores to do. There was always house-work and needlework to attend to or something cooking that needed attention on the big stove.

"Mam," she asked her mother one day after school, "have you ever gone away from Cork?"

"No," her mother smiled. "I was born in Cork, like my own parents, and 'tis here I shall probably die. But my brothers have travelled the world."

"Tell me everythin'," Margaret begged. She loved her mother's stories about their family.

"Hush, girl. You've chores to be gettin' done," said her mother, knowing their conversation would go on now for some time.

"Please Mam," Margaret persisted. "Just one story. I can help with the cookin' while you talk."

Their talks always began this way, and despite her show of reluctance, Mary Anne Bulkley enjoyed telling her daughter about their family's history. It was good for the child to know her past. Besides, thought Mary Anne, it was all Margaret would ever know of life outside Cork. In a few years' time she would put away her dreams of exotic places. She would marry and begin a family of her own. Why not let the girl dream a little before then?

"Well now," Mary Anne began—and spun again her familiar tales.

⬥⬥⬥

John Barry, Margaret's grandfather, was a sailor but gave up the sea when he married Juliana Reardon, likely around 1740. He worked as a bricklayer for many years and during this time, the Barry family grew. Their first child, born on October 11, 1741, was named James. He was followed by Redmond, Patrick and John. The youngest, and the only girl, was Mary Anne—Margaret's mother. Mary Anne couldn't remember the birth dates of her three other brothers, but they were not close in age.

James Barry, in his teen years, worked with his father as a

hod carrier, hauling portable platforms for the bricks and mortar needed in construction. Around the time Mary Anne was born, her father left bricklaying to become the owner or manager of a public house called The Neptune—one of a number of taverns that lined the roadsides. Steep stone stairs placed at intervals along the river's edge led up to the cobbled road along the riverbank. Barry's pub stood near one of these stairways. When John became a pubkeeper, his son James also gave up bricks and mortar and turned his hand to sign painting. It was James' sign that welcomed visitors to the pub. As John loved to point out, it was a grand sign with King Neptune himself on one side and the sailing ship *Neptune* on the other. John was proud of both the sign and his son.

Later John left the Neptune to become vintner at the Brazen-Head Tavern on Henry Street in Hamon's Marsh, another suburb of Cork. But the call of the sea was too much for him, and he left the tavern to become a crossing trader—a person who carried trade goods between England and Ireland. His family remained in Cork.

Like their mother, the Barry children were ardent Catholics. Their father was Protestant. The marriage was something of a scandal in both families because Catholics and Protestants were not friendly politically, but John and Juliana seemed happy.

Of Mary Anne's four brothers, only one was captured in a formal portrait. James was painted several times during his life by fellow artists. He was a handsome youth whose hair glowed like copper streaked with sunlight, but his most striking feature was his bright blue eyes, full of life and promise.

When Mary Anne was of age, she married a merchant named Jeremiah Bulkley, who was originally from Dublin. They made their home in Cork and had three children, two daughters and a son. The boy was named John, after Mary Anne's favourite brother. One of the daughters passed away at a very young age, leaving Margaret Anne as the only surviving girl in the family. Margaret had her mother's fair complexion and red hair, but her penchant for asking questions was not a family trait. Margaret always giggled at this part of the story.

"Tell me about Uncle John," Margaret begged.

Mary Anne repeated her stories about the girl's uncles. John, her youngest brother, was the handsomest of all. "He sang like a nightingale," Mary Anne told Margaret, "and could melt your heart with his smile. He was my very best friend."

Margaret never knew her Uncle John. He had died before she was born, but he lived in her imagination. When she was younger, she sometimes confused him in her mind with her brother, John. At times she even thought little John was her mother's favourite because he was so like the other John.

The next uncle was Patrick. He enlisted in the Third Division of Marines at Bristol. Soon after, he deserted and joined the East India Company. As a deserter he had to conceal his identity. He adopted his grandmother's maiden name, Reardon, changing the spelling slightly and signing himself "Patrick Riordan." Patrick did well with the company and spent fourteen years in its service. Like his father, Patrick had very fine handwriting and for awhile was secretary to Captain Gordon, who in turn was *aide-de-camp* to the head of the company, Governor Mackpherson. Then an accident left Patrick's hand so badly injured he could no longer perform his secretarial duties. No one knew if Captain Gordon found another job for him—one that required only one good hand. A letter dated 1802 from Redmond to James speaks as though Patrick were dead, but in September 1808 Patrick was preparing for an expedition to the West Indies. No one heard from Patrick again but Mary Anne believed he remained in the West Indies.

Redmond, too, served with the East India Company, but as a seaman on the *Hound*, a sloop of war. Margaret wasn't sure what a sloop-of-war was, but it sounded dangerous and exciting. Her mother said the East India Company was very old. It began in 1600 with a series of trading posts, or factories, all along the coast of Asia and the lands lying between the Cape of Good Hope and the Straits of Magellan. These factories were far away and largely unprotected, so they were vulnerable to raiders and pirates who roamed the area. To protect its valuable trade, the company formed the Bombay Marine, its own fighting navy. Margaret shivered at the thought. Even the words had a wonderful ring: the Bombay Marine! In her imagination, Margaret pictured her uncle standing on the deck of his ship, tanned and barefoot, winning battles at sea all around East India.

Mary Anne knew that Margaret's vision of her uncle didn't match reality. Redmond hated life aboard ship and wanted his release so he could return to his trade as a bricklayer. In the 1780s, on board the *Hound*, near Sheerness, he wrote his brother James to ask for help. But the only way he could obtain his release was by purchasing a substitute—hiring someone to take his place. On March 9, 1785, serving on the *Cumberland*, he sent another letter to his brother, pleading again for help but to no avail.

Margaret's favourite stories were about her Uncle James Barry. His paintings hung in important galleries, and in grand homes and castles in Europe and England. "Tell me about Uncle James and Edmund Burke," she demanded.

James began as a painter of signs, then studied with the landscape painter John Butts. The great Irish statesman, Edmund Burke, noticed Uncle James' work. It was a turning point in his career. Under Burke's sponsorship, Uncle James studied in Italy and Switzerland. When he returned to London, Burke introduced him to friends who gave him his first commissions. His fame grew and he was admitted to the Royal Academy of Art. He was a talented portrait painter but preferred his huge historical paintings and did only a few portraits—mostly for members of Burke's family and close friends.

Margaret's uncle's paintings were outstanding on many counts, not the least of which were the historical subjects themselves. He did not limit himself to classical themes but depicted current events as well. In 1776 he produced the famous *Death of General Wolfe,* and he may have travelled to Canada to do preliminary sketches.

Uncle James used his fame and art to draw people's attention to important issues. He wanted to educate the public about art and published four major books on the subject. He also supported the abolition of Ireland's cruel penal laws and promoted the acceptance of Catholics as full citizens.

The penal laws were the result of a battle between church and state. In 1536, Henry VIII broke with the Catholic church and was named head of the newly formed Protestant Church of England. The Catholic religion was declared null and void. In 1541, Henry was named King of Ireland and created the Church of Ireland, the Irish counterpart to the Church of England. To "encourage" the Irish to convert from their Catholic faith, strict laws were passed dealing with everything from the value of property Catholics could own (very small) to the kinds of jobs they could hold (very menial). Violations carried severe penalties. In 1571, Queen Elizabeth I imposed more restrictions, including harsh penalties for those who refused to attend Sabbath services at the Church of Ireland. In every way possible, Catholics in Ireland were repressed and stripped of opportunity. It was a cruel and vicious program designed to grind them into submission.

These laws were still in effect in Uncle James' day although their impact had lessened in England, where the

Irish were needed as soldiers and labourers. In Ireland, however, the laws were still in full force, and from his safe haven in London, Uncle James fought against them. Along with equality and justice, upholding Roman Catholicism became a central theme in the painter's life and art.

Margaret had never met her Uncle James. Once he left Ireland he never returned. The family did not usually keep in close touch with one another. When John died, James learned of his brother's death from a friend, not from his family. He did not return for the burial. Still, her mother's stories made him real for the little girl. It was exciting to have a famous relative.

"Did he ever give you one of his paintings?" she asked her mother.

"Now why ever would he do that?" she replied. "There's hundreds of people payin' thousands of pounds for those pictures. So he'd not be after sendin' one to a little sister he hardly remembers.

"No, I've not even seen his famous pictures. But I did see the signs he painted—like the one that hung over my own father's public house. That was how Edmund Burke noticed him, you know. My brother was lucky to have Mr. Burke for a friend."

"What excitin' lives my uncles have," the little girl sighed. "Men do such interestin' things. Sometimes the sisters at the convent tell us stories about famous people, but they're almost always about men."

Mary Anne smiled at her daughter. "Women's lives can be excitin'. It's just that we do different things than men do. Just be after thinkin' for a minute: how would I ever have such a fine family if I'd been traipsin' off to Switzerland and Italy or India or the Caribbean like my brothers? Sure, if I'd been gallivantin' like them, you and your brother wouldn't be here today!"

"Ah Mam," Margaret sighed. "You know what I mean."

Her mother smiled again. "Indeed I do. I sometimes felt the same as you when I was a little girl. But even though it isn't always excitin', some women have very special lives. Look at Nano Nagle, herself as founded your very school. No one could do better than Nano Nagle. 'Twas like a blessed saint she was."

Mary Anne paused, thinking again of the remarkable achievements of this one woman who had defied authority because of her convictions. Her persistent efforts brought education to the Catholic children of Cork and eased the suffering of the children of the poor.

"That reminds me. I talked with the sisters the other day. They say you're doin' very well in class."

Margaret loved the classes given by the Presentation Order of Nuns. They were held in Cork in a new convent building on Douglas Street. The school was remarkable for the fact that it existed at all. The cruel fingers of the penal laws had wound themselves into the education of Catholic children, restricting the type of education they could receive and the subjects they could study.

Nano Nagle was a relative of Edmund Burke, the Irish statesman and writer who had been such a friend to Margaret's Uncle James. Like Burke, Nano Nagle wanted to help the downtrodden Irish. She turned her efforts to the children of the poor. She knew what it was to be shunned and persecuted. She had been born in Dublin to parents who were active Jacobites. Jacobites believed that James II, who had been on the British throne in the late 1600s, was the true king and that his descendants were the true heirs to the throne. They were called traitors for these beliefs.

In 1728 Nagle was sent to France for an education. Five years later she returned to Ireland and attempted to set up a school for impoverished Catholic children in Dublin. The task was overwhelming, and Nagle was unable to continue her work. She returned to France and entered a convent but did not stay long. After the death of her sister, Anne, Nano Nagle returned to Ireland. In 1754 or 1755 she opened a school for girls in a mud cabin on Cove Lane in Cork. Finding ways to subvert the hated penal laws, Nagle continued her work, and within a few years, two hundred girls attended her school. By 1760 there were seven schools in Cork for Catholic children, five for girls and two for boys, each providing a rudimentary education along with religious instruction.

Nagle introduced the order of the Ursuline Nuns in 1771. Four years later she founded a society devoted to the poor. The building that housed Margaret's school was begun in 1775. Nagle continued her work until her death in Cork on April 26, 1784. After her death the order she founded became known as the Presentation Order of Nuns. This was the order that ran the convent school Margaret attended.

Education was precious to the girl, as it was to most Catholic children in Ireland. She learned quickly and remembered her lessons well.

With thoughts of Nano Nagle and her family's past swirling in her head, Margaret finished the last of her preparations for supper. She knew her conversation with her mother was at an end. Soon her father and brother would be home, and they would share the evening meal over talk of today, not of far-off people and places. But Margaret didn't mind. There would be time for talk with her mother another day.

❧❧❧

"Margaret, you'll have to write this letter for me," her mother said one day. "'Tis the palsy in my hands that's gettin' worse and worse now. I can hardly hold a cup, much less a pen. I will tell you what to say, and you can write it for me."

Margaret was proud of her handwriting. It wasn't as good

as her father's or her Uncle Patrick's, but it was much better than her brother John's, which was quick and careless. As her mother dictated, Margaret carefully wrote her rough copy on a piece of scrap paper, then went back to make corrections. Her mother read the draft over carefully and nodded her head. "That'll do fine," she said.

Margaret used a small whetstone to sharpen the blade on her little penknife, then cut a fresh goose quill, paying close attention to the cut so there were no ragged edges to splatter the ink. Carefully she recopied the letter on a fresh sheet of paper. When it was done she picked up a small ceramic jar, put her hand carefully over the holes in its pewter lid and shook it briskly. The jar held dry sand. Shaking it broke up any lumps. Then she sprinkled sand over the letter to blot the wet ink and prevent smudging. Once the ink was dry, she unscrewed the lid and carefully tipped the sand back into the jar.

Writing letters for her mother made Margaret feel grown up and important although Mary Anne fretted about keeping information in the letters private.

"You've to remember this is family business," she told her daughter. "You're not to be after tellin' anybody about what's in my letters."

"No Mam, I won't," Margaret promised. "I'm good at keeping secrets."

Her brother, too, was good at keeping secrets. Like Margaret, John was dazzled by thoughts of his uncles' seafaring adventures. Now he astonished the family by announcing a new plan.

"I'm to be a Royal Marine," he boasted.

Margaret's imagination ran wild when he set sail for the West Indies.

"Write to me often," John told his sister as he left the little cottage in Cork.

"I will. Oh, I will," she promised. "And you must write to me. Tell me all about the wonderful places you see. Maybe you'll even find Uncle Redmond or Uncle Patrick."

John laughed. "Perhaps," he said. "But don't forget—I'm a marine, not a trader. I won't have much time to be sittin' around takin' tea with the locals."

Margaret missed him. She remembered all the good times they'd had and some of the not-so-good times as well. John knew just what to say to make her angry, and he'd laugh when she got scolded for losing her temper. Still, life was more peaceful when he was gone. It seemed he was forever getting into scraps, and sometimes it was all her mother could do to talk her father into forgiving him "just this once."

"I wish I could be a marine, too," she told her mother.

"Sure now, and that's as silly a thing as I've ever heard," her mother laughed. "When you grow up you'll marry a good man and become a proper wife and mother. Wait till I tell your father you want to be a lady marine!"

"Well, not exactly a marine," Margaret sputtered. "But I'd like to travel the world as John is doing. Why can't I see the West Indies, too?"

"No reason at all," her mother replied. "It takes a great deal of money to travel, but if you marry someone with wealth, there's no reason why you can't—if he allows you to go, that is."

❧❧❧

Margaret looked forward to exciting letters from her brother, but the letters that arrived weren't about his travels and his adventures. Like his uncle, John didn't like life at sea and sent plaintive letters home. Like his uncle, he wanted to buy his way out of his enlistment. John begged his parents to give him the money that would set him free.

Somehow they scraped up the money, and soon John was back in Cork. When he could not find work that suited him, his parents apprenticed him to an attorney in Dublin. The law was a fine career for a young man. John found not only his career but also the woman he wanted to wed. Her name was Kate Ward, and his letters home were ecstatic.

"She's wealthy," he wrote and added that she loved him dearly. They wanted to marry, but there was a problem. Kate was an orphan who lived with an older brother. The brother looked after her affairs and refused to allow her to marry someone who didn't have a piece of property to his name.

John proposed a simple solution to his problem. If his parents set him up with some land and a house, Kate's brother could no longer refuse the match. It would be expensive, but, as John pointed out, it would cost almost nothing compared to the money that Kate Ward would bring to the marriage. Her fortune would be his. Further, it would help his career. Kate's friends were wealthy, too, and they could bring a lot of business to a young lawyer.

Jeremiah and Mary Anne were proud of their clever and ambitious son, and pleased that a wealthy heiress would consider marrying into the family. But Jeremiah had doubts about settling such a large amount on their son.

"I think we should do it," Mary Anne told Jeremiah.

"But we don't have enough money," he replied.

"We don't have cash, but you have a good business. You could borrow against it."

Jeremiah nodded slowly. He had done well since he started the grocery store. Business was good and promised to increase. It was true that he could mortgage the business and let John use the money to set himself up. Still, a thread of doubt wove through his thoughts.

"Look now," Mary Anne said, "he says himself that he'll have control of Kate's fortune once they're married. So he'll be able to pay us back quickly. We won't have the mortgage for long. And he is our son, after all."

Reluctantly Jeremiah had to agree. He was their son. Surely he would look after their interests and keep his promise. He agreed. True to his word, Jeremiah mortgaged the store for as much as he could and sent the money to John. It took John no time at all to set himself up in Dublin and begin courting Kate Ward.

Margaret sighed at the romance of it all. She pictured the wedding, asking her mother endless questions about her own wedding and imagining the grand life ahead for her brother and his bride. In her mind's eye she could already see the fine home with its lovely furnishings and rows of eager servants tending to Kate and John's every wish. Surely they'd ask her to come to Dublin for a visit—a long visit.

Mary Anne shook her head at Margaret's imagination. Give her a thread and she'd imagine a whole garment. Still, Margaret was better off dreaming about weddings and women's things than dreaming about being a marine, thought Mary Anne.

Soon after, Jeremiah had some pressing debts at the store and asked John for some of the money back to clear off his bills. John refused. Jeremiah could hardly believe what happened next. He was taken to debtor's court and thrown into prison in Dublin. He could not keep up payments on his mortgage and lost everything he had put up in security. His home, his business and his belongings were seized by the courts. John had completely turned his back on his father and family. His mother and sister were left alone with no means of supporting themselves. Still John refused to help. Mary Anne was stunned and Margaret was bitter. In their wildest dreams neither had ever imagined a situation like this.

Saddened, Mary Anne considered her future. Two years earlier, in June of 1804, she had sent her daughter to London to visit with Mary Anne's cousin, Daniel Reardon. While Margaret was there, Mary Anne had hoped she could visit with her famous uncle as well. Not only was it an opportunity for James to meet his niece, but there was the chance he could introduce her to some of his artist friends and make her welcome in London.

It was not to be. When Margaret returned home, Mary Anne learned that James had ignored his niece. Furious, she had written to him, listing her grievances. "What did you give my Child when she was here last June. Did you ask her to Dinner, in short did you act as an Uncle, or as a Christian to a poor unprotected unprovided for Girl?" she railed. James never replied to his sister's letter. As inhospitable as he had seemed at the time, it now appeared that Mary Anne's famous brother might be her last hope of staying out of the poorhouse.

Chapter Two

LONDON

"WE'LL HAVE TO GO TO LONDON and see my brother James," she told her daughter. "He's a wealthy man. He should be able to help us. He's never married, so mayhap I can be his housekeeper. Surely a famous man like that will be able to find some place in his household for his poor sister and his only niece."

When the women arrived at Barry's home on Castle Street in London, they discovered his true situation and the reason he had ignored Margaret's earlier visit. He was ill, suffering from a disease that was probably acromegaly. Mary Anne had not known about her brother's illness, nor, in its early stages, did his friends. Acromegaly is a condition that affects not only the body but often the mind as well. The physical symptoms are a coarsening of the features, lengthening of the nose and jutting of the chin. It begins slowly with almost no physical effects. They appear gradually after the victim reaches middle age. It is a painful disease, caused by an overactive pituitary gland, and leaves its victims with grinding headaches, impaired vision and heart problems. At times it also creates a dangerous paranoia, a persecution mania. Today it can be treated, but in Barry's day its causes were not even suspected. Acromegaly may have been responsible for the change in Barry's personality from the friendly, outgoing and popular young man he had been to the warped, quarrelsome old recluse he became in later years. In the grip of his paranoia he fought and argued with friends, patrons, sponsors and clients, one by one reducing his circle of friends to the very few who could understand and put up with his problems.

Once the darling of the art world, Barry was now cast out of the Royal Academy. Gallery owners refused to show his paintings, or they kept them in back rooms and out-of-the-way corners. Wealthy patrons no longer sought his services, and he no longer had commissions to fill. With no income, he fought to continue painting his heroic themes by stripping himself of possessions to buy art supplies. Instead of the lively salon that once surrounded his studio, James, after alienating his friends, moved to a shabby house at 36 Castle Street, where he lived his lonely life. He even fired the maid who cleaned his house, believing her to be a thief, and never replaced her. With no one to clean, his house became dirtier and more unkempt every day.

He was in desperate straits and physically, emotionally and financially unable to offer anything to anyone. When Mary Anne saw her brother's house, it was obvious that the squalor and poverty were nothing new. He had lived in these conditions for years. She now understood why her famous brother had not come home for their brother's or even their father's funeral. He was ashamed to let his family see him in this condition. That same pride must have caused him to refuse his inheritance.

"Goodness knows he could have used it," Mary Anne whispered to herself, "but he was so proud he would never let on."

Not only was he as badly off as they were, he was seriously ill as well. He could not help them nor did he want them to stay.

"Mam, I'm sorry he's sick, but I wouldn't want to stay in this house anyway," Margaret whispered to her mother. "I've never seen anyone who lives as he does. He's got just one blanket, and it's nailed to the side of his bed. The house and yard are full of trash and garbage, and it stinks from all his paints and turpentine. It's cold and musty besides," she said, shivering and trying to choke back her tears.

"I know, love," her mother replied. "It isn't what I expected to find either."

Wearily they set off to find Mary Anne's cousin, Daniel Reardon, and his family at 2 Corbet Court on Grace Church Street.

As they walked, Mary Anne made plans. "We can only stay with Daniel for a short time," she told Margaret. "His house is small enough as it is. We'll have to find lodgings of our own as soon as we can."

Margaret nodded but could not imagine how that might happen. Lodgings cost money, and she knew they didn't have any. She decided it would be up to her to help look after her mother and to find a job somewhere that would pay for their room and board.

Once Daniel had made them welcome, Margaret turned to him. "Uncle Daniel, can you help me find a position? I could be a governess. I can read and write, and I can do sums quite well. Or perhaps I could be a housemaid somewhere."

"I'll see what I can find," her uncle promised.

Soon after, he heard of a place that might suit her. "There's a lady in Camden Town who needs a maid," he told his niece. "Why don't you write and apply?"

Happily, Margaret sent off the letter but soon learned she was expected to live in the house. Her mother would not be able to live with her, and the wages were so low she couldn't afford to pay room and board elsewhere for her mother.

"I wish I could find some sort of work," Mary Anne sighed. "It's a heavy load for your young shoulders to bear. But my poor hands are so shaky now there's nothin' at all I can do. No one would hire a poor old woman like me."

"Don't worry, Mam," Margaret smiled. "Something will come up. And if it comes to that, I could always go into the mills."

Mary Anne shook her head. "No, I don't think you could. You're too old now for the mills. They only want young children to work with the spinning. And they don't pay enough to keep a body alive."

"If I were a man I could be a soldier," she told her mother.

"Aye. And if a pig had wings it could fly," Mary Anne replied. "You aren't a man, so there's no good thinkin' about what you could do if you were."

But the notion tantalized Margaret. She knew that a few women had pretended to be men. Some had even succeeded for a time. Margaret had heard stories about women like Hannah Snell, who called herself James Grey and in the 1740s joined Frazier's Marines. And there was Ann Mills, who served on board the British frigate *Maidstone* until her true identity was discovered.

There were others as well. Mary Dixon spent sixteen years in the British army before doctors, treating her for a musket wound, discovered she was really a woman. Sally St. Claire was killed in action in America while serving with the army, and Deborah Sampson Gannett, who enlisted under the name Robert Shurleff, was an excellent soldier. Only when she became ill did doctors discovered she certainly wasn't a man. There were songs and ballads about other women who followed sweethearts and lovers into the army, but they were quickly discovered and sent home.

"I guess that's not the solution to our problem," Margaret admitted.

On February 22, 1806, when it appeared there was nothing for Mary Anne and Margaret but Daniel Reardon's continued charity or the poorhouse, James Barry died of pleuritic fever.

Barry had some powerful friends, and while many had

turned away from him over the years, two remained loyal to the end. The Earl of Buchan and General Francisco de Miranda had been Barry's friends for many years. Buchan continued to visit Barry and was increasingly distressed by his situation. It was Buchan who began a subscription for Barry, collecting sums from different friends, until £1,000 was amassed. The fund was entrusted to Sir Robert Peel, the member of parliament for Lancaster. Peel bought an annuity in Barry's name, which would guarantee him £250 per year, paid quarterly—enough to enable Barry to continue his work and to live at a reasonable level of comfort.

But it came too late. Before Barry received even the first instalment of the annuity, he died. Barry had been a well-known figure, and despite his recent troubles his art testified to his greatness. The honours that had eroded over the years were restored. On March 14, 1806, Mary Anne and her daughter joined members of the art world at Barry's funeral and saw him buried in the crypt of St. Paul's Cathedral. Ironically he was placed beside the man who had been a friend, mentor and, later, bitter enemy, Sir Joshua Reynolds.

Peel, who was the trustee of Barry's annuity fund, contributed £200 towards the cost of the funeral and a memorial tablet. An even finer tribute came from General Miranda's mistress. Barry had been her best friend, she said. He gave her the best of advice at all times, and he loved and admired her son, Leander.

Few of Barry's former associates knew of Mary Anne and Margaret's existence. He rarely spoke of his family, and many were unaware he had brothers and a sister. But when Buchan and Miranda met Mary Anne, they were shocked to learn she was penniless and desperate.

Privately Mary Anne must have grieved for the £1000 that had been raised for her brother but that now, under the terms of the annuity, was lost to the family. "It doesn't seem right somehow," she told Margaret. "The money was raised for my brother, but he never enjoyed a penny of it, and now we can't touch it either."

Barry might not have had money, but he was not as destitute as he appeared. He left behind a number of finished paintings as well as some etchings. Two of the paintings were in his well-known large historical mode. Barry had not made a will—or if he had, no one knew where it was. Before anything could be done with the paintings, Mary Anne had to find out who was entitled to share in Barry's estate.

"You would be wise to move while your brother's name is still on everyone's lips," Daniel advised her. "The sooner the pictures can be disposed of, the better."

"I'm not knowin' about paintin's and etchin's and such like," she said, "but the gentlemen said they could be valuable. Sure and the money would be a godsend, but I've no idea how to set about sellin' them. If you could help me, Daniel, I'll do whatever you say."

While Mary Anne was busy looking after her brother's affairs, Margaret began to think about her own future. She talked openly with Lord Buchan and General Miranda, searching for a solution to her problem.

"I don't have a dowry, so I won't even be able to make a good marriage," she told them. "I don't have a religious calling, so I can't join a convent. I guess I don't really have anything to look forward to at all."

"But you do, you know," the general replied. "You're young, you're intelligent and you're a good worker. You could do whatever you wanted."

Before she could stop herself, Margaret's temper flared. "Maybe it seems that way to you because you're a man, but I *can't* do anythin' I want. I'm just a girl. I can't be an accountant or an attorney or a soldier or a doctor or anythin' else. I'm not educated or trained to do anythin'. And, as if things aren't bad enough, I'm Irish besides. Most people here don't want Irish girls to be anythin' but scullery maids."

Miranda looked at her thoughtfully for a moment. "Why do you have to be Irish?"

Startled, Margaret could only stare at him and stutter, "Why? B-b-b-because it's what I am. That's why!"

"But my dear girl, the only way people can tell you're Irish is by your accent. If you want to be a governess or a lady's maid, lose your accent. Then you can tell people you are from London, and they need know nothing more than that unless you choose to inform them."

Margaret's eyes gleamed. "Could I? Could I really do that?"

The smallest of smiles touched Miranda's lips as he raised his eyebrows and tipped his head towards her. "I think you could if you really wanted to."

"But how can I begin? How can I learn to talk like a Londoner?"

Now the general allowed himself a chuckle. He leaned forward, placed his forefinger across his lips, then touched the lobe of his ear. "Listen. That's all you have to do. When I was in America, I wanted to be taken as an American. I learned from the people around me, just as you must do. They will be your tutors. Listen to them talk. Everywhere you go—in the shops, on the streets—listen to how people speak. Never mind what they're saying, just listen to how they say it. Then see if you can shape your words the way they do.

"And if you want an education, all you have to do is read. For that you would be welcome to use my library. You know where I live: 27 Grafton Street. I will tell my housekeeper, Sarah Andrews, that you are to have free use of my books. My work takes me away from time to time, but my books are always there.

"If you're serious, little Margaret, if those aren't just empty words, then perhaps we can find something worthwhile for you to do."

Flabbergasted, Margaret watched the general walk away.

Words whirled around in her mind. "If I'm serious! General Miranda, you have no idea how serious I can be. I do have a mind. I know I can learn. And you're going to be surprised at just how well I can learn."

Margaret walked back to the Reardon home in a daze, almost as though she were sleepwalking. She took no notice of where her feet led her, paid no attention to the sights and sounds around her. All she could hear were the general's words: "Perhaps we can find something worthwhile for you to do." She repeated them over and over in her mind like a mantra. Something worthwhile to do. She had no idea what that might mean, but she felt she could put her trust in General Miranda. "Maybe there is a future for Mam and me after all," she whispered to herself. "Maybe things will get better." The first thing to do was learn to speak English instead of Irish. And she could begin this very day.

❦❦❦

Margaret's feet hurt. It felt as though she had been walking on cobblestone pavement forever. Her thin shoes were scant protection against the irregular stones, and she was painfully aware of several bruises. Hunger cramped her stomach and thirst pulled at her mouth and throat. The morning rain left puddles that dragged at the hem of her dress and seeped into her shoes and stockings. Even when the sun broke through, spray from passing carriages and drays coated her clothing and left grime on her hands and face. She and her mother dodged pots of waste and night water tossed from overhead windows with only the warning cry of "Gardeloo!" *(Guardez l'eau*)* to send them scurrying against the nearest wall. She was tired of trudging up and down the uneven

*watch out for the water

stones, skirting along the crooked streets and narrow alleys.

"Mam, aren't you gettin' tired?"

Her mother sighed. "Indeed, Margaret, 'tis very tired I am. But we're overdue to find a place to stay. Daniel's been kindness itself, but he has barely room enough for his own family, never mind two extras."

"And are lodgin's that expensive?" Margaret asked.

"I guess they're not expensive for London, but they're more than I'd pay in Cork. My brother's friends, the general and the earl, advanced me a bit of money against the sale of his paintin's, but I've to repay every penny of it. That's why I can't afford to be wastin' any of it."

"Will you be sellin' the paintings soon?"

"That I don't know," her mother replied. "'Tis my guess that I'll be after sellin' them just as soon as I find someone who's after wantin' them."

Mary Anne still hoped to get a good price for her brother's paintings as soon as the question of his will was settled, but she quickly discovered it was not easy to sell such large pictures. Daniel suggested placing them with a gallery, but the gallery owners asked a high commission for handling such works. Mary Anne wanted to keep as much of the money for herself as she could. This was her only hedge against the poorhouse. Meanwhile the earl tried to help her find buyers.

Today she had other concerns. She and Margaret had to find their own place to stay. Daniel was her cousin, but they had never been close friends. It was generous of him to take them in at all, and she did not want to stay longer than was absolutely necessary. Mary Anne and her daughter tried to help Daniel's wife around the house, but she was frequently reminded of the old Irish proverb, "Two women can no more share a kitchen than two hens can share a nest." It would be best if they left while they were still in her cousin's good graces.

She never guessed it would be so hard to find a place to stay. Many of the big old houses had cards in the window advertising rooms to let, but when Mary Anne trudged up to the doors and rang the bells, landladies shook their heads as soon as they heard Mary Anne talk.

"No. No vacancies. We don't take Irish here."

Others didn't seem to mind that they were Irish but wouldn't take single women.

Now they walked on in silence. The weary hours ran one into another and still they trudged up one street and down the next. It was the same story in each block. The rooms were too expensive. The landlady didn't take women. There were no rooms for Irish. It was hard to imagine that out of all the rooms for rent in the great city of London, there were none open to Mary Anne and her daughter.

In the distance, they heard the peal of a church bell.

"Sure and if I'm not after bein' the silly goose," Mary Anne sputtered. "That's the end of town where we've to look for rooms. That's where we'll find our own kind."

"Do you think so, Mam?"

"There's not a shadow of a doubt," Mary Anne smiled. "Come along. We'll have our own place before the goin' down of the sun."

It wasn't quite as easy as Mary Anne hoped. They went back to Daniel Reardon's house for yet another night. The next day Mary Anne led the way to a neighbourhood that Daniel suggested. It was a poor neighbourhood, but it was near a Catholic church and women did take in lodgers. On the streets she heard people speaking in the familiar accents of Ireland.

"Sure and 'twill be almost like bein' at home," Mary Anne smiled.

They found a warm welcome in the home of a cheerful widow from Rosslaire, a village not far from Cork on Ireland's south coast, and settled cosily into their new home—a shared bedroom and a small sitting room. The widow's lodgers were served breakfast and tea in the dining room. Those were the two main meals of the day. Mary Anne and Margaret could make do with that. And the price was reasonable.

Once she had a place to stay, Mary Anne turned her attention back to the business at hand. She offered many prayers that she could find a wealthy buyer. With a little luck her brother's estate might give them what Barry himself had been unable to provide: some sort of income and a chance to make a life for themselves.

Mary Anne thought long and hard before she made up her mind. It was not an easy decision to make, but she convinced herself it was the only logical move. She would abandon Jeremiah and do what she could to protect Margaret.

It was a confusing time for Margaret. She could only watch while her mother agonized over a number of difficult decisions. At first Margaret thought they would take whatever money they got for her uncle's paintings and go home again to Ireland. "But look, darlin'," Mary Anne pointed out. "If we do that the bailiffs can seize the money to pay your father's debts. We'd be left without a penny."

Jeremiah wrote from prison to his son, John, and to his daughter, Margaret. Mary Anne refused to let her daughter answer the letters. She did not want Jeremiah to know where they were. She did not know that John, for his own reasons, also ignored his father's letters.

Later, when Jeremiah was released from prison, he remained in Dublin. He picked up his mail from 38 Fishamble Street, but he lived elsewhere. He continued searching for his family. He knew his wife and daughter were together, and a friend told him they had been seen in London. Jeremiah sent a number of letters to his daughter in care of Daniel Reardon, guessing that Mary Anne would be in touch with her cousin. He complained to Reardon that he had not heard from his wife or daughter for a long while and that he was worried about them. Reardon protected Mary Anne's privacy and did not tell Jeremiah her new address. Jeremiah remained in London and never managed to make contact with his wife or daughter again.

With the question of lodgings solved, Mary Anne was now able to deal with another problem. Her brother had died without a will. She applied to the courts in London for permission to look after his affairs. At first she claimed to be a widow. When she could not produce the papers to prove this, she reluctantly admitted she was still married and her husband was in debtor's prison in Ireland.

This time she was in luck. There was no sympathy in London for the problems of the Irish. The court in London felt no need to concern itself with matters before the Irish courts. Nor did it feel obligated to inform anyone in Ireland that Mary Anne might come into enough money to clear her husband's name. The permission Mary Anne needed was given, and she was appointed executor of James Barry's estate.

It was difficult for a woman to do business or to look after legal affairs. At that time women had almost no legal rights. Everything they had belonged to their husbands. If their husbands died or could not support them, there were few places to turn for assistance. There were none of the welfare systems, social services, pensions or income supplements that are available today. If Mary Anne could not find a way to make some money from her brother's estate, she could still be sent to the poorhouse. She worried about herself, but she worried even more about Margaret. She could not depend on John to look after his sister, and the girl had no other close relatives she could turn to for help.

Barry's fame and his fine public funeral spread word of his death farther than Mary Anne might have wished. At the time of James' death their brother, Redmond, was listed on the rolls of the Suffolk Prison Ship *Portsmouth* as an invalid. When he learned of his brother's death, he immediately contacted his cousin, Daniel Reardon, asking about his brother's estate. Daniel showed the letter to Mary Anne.

It was difficult for Mary Anne to know exactly what Redmond's situation was at that point. He may have been injured in action or stricken by illness. He may have been assigned to light duty on the prison ship. Service on prison ships was not desirable, but it was easier than service at sea and at least provided him with food and shelter. Prison ships often were used to hold convicted criminals awaiting deportation.

"I doubt that's my brother's handwriting," she replied to Daniel. "I don't recognize it." She had hardened herself to Redmond's plea and refused to give him a share.

Angrily Redmond complained to Daniel Reardon of Mary Anne's treatment. He was as entitled to part of James' estate as she was, he told Daniel, but she was trying to claim it all. Redmond was bitter, but Mary Anne was desperate.

"Sellin' me brother's work is much harder than I thought it would be," she told her daughter. "Now it looks as though everyone is goin' to be askin' for part of the few pennies I'll get."

Privately Mary Anne worried that if Redmond appeared, Patrick might also claim a share of the estate. Would her son, John, try to claim a share as well? Finally, in order to keep Redmond silent, Mary Anne arranged to have someone pay the fifteen guineas needed to gain Redmond's release from the marines, and on September 11, 1806, he disappeared from their lives.

During this time Mary Anne and her daughter were kept busy sorting out James Barry's effects, packing up and selling everything that might bring in a few coppers while storing away such things as the plates for James' etchings. Margaret worked beside her mother, sifting through mounds of material.

James had lived at 36 Castle Street East since the autumn of 1788. Year by year the house had become more dilapidated and run down. Margaret and her mother had to cope with years of neglect, along with the filth and debris, as they searched through the clutter in James' living quarters and studio. It was hard to know what could be sold.

"Mam, I know someone might buy his sketch pads and such, but what about this palette? Surely it's too worn and dirty to bother about?"

Mary Anne studied the shaped wooden board in her daughter's hands. It was crusted with layers of old paint. "I wouldn't give a ha'penny for it," she agreed. "But someone might want it. Just put it to one side."

His brushes, they agreed, should be worth something. Several jugs had brushes crammed in them any which way—fat brushes, thin brushes, brushes of all shapes and sizes. There were boxes of old pigment blocks to consider as well. Artists bought their colours in blocks, then ground the pigment and mixed it with linseed oil and turpentine to make paint. Some of James' pigment blocks were almost new while others were just crumbled rusks. A mixture of completed and half-completed paintings leaned against the walls. Some were on canvas, others on board. Mary Anne was perplexed and unsure of what she might do with them.

"Don't worry about them," Buchan told her. "These artist fellows just paint one picture over another if they don't like the first one. Someone will buy the boards and canvas and paint his own pictures on top of them."

James' clothing posed another problem. There was little to begin with, and most was so worn and tattered it didn't seem it could even be used for rags. At first Redmond had insisted he should have all of James' clothing. James' shoes, too, were so cracked and broken and covered with splotches of paint it was hard to imagine they could be useful to anyone. "I wish he could have seen what he was *gearán** about," Mary Anne grumbled. "It would serve him right if I gave them to him."

There was very little furniture in the house to sell. They could sell his bed and his paint-splattered table along with a few chairs, but there was little more. It was obvious he had already sold most of his possessions to buy the paints he needed.

As Margaret and her mother sorted through James' household, they learned other things about the famous painter. He was not well liked by his neighbours. Young boys and ruffians made a game of shouting taunts at his door, throwing stones at the house and tossing garbage in the yard. Dead cats, rotten potatoes, smelly fish-heads and more lay in untidy heaps. James had not had the time, energy or will to clear them away, so they stayed until the neighbours complained. His windows, broken long ago, were stuffed with old rags to keep out the wind and rain. Despite this, the mist and dampness crept in, spreading a layer of mildew on the wall hangings. Everywhere they turned, the house reeked of poverty and neglect.

Margaret and Mary Anne wanted to finish as quickly as possible so they could leave. The landlord was already looking for new tenants, and Mary Anne didn't want to have to pay the extra rent that would be due if they stayed beyond the end of James' lease.

With hard work the clutter was soon cleared away. Her brother's paintings, art supplies and etchings were stored in Mary Anne's tiny sitting room. The household furnishings were sold. A rag and scrap man came by, exchanging a few coins for the bits and pieces left behind.

Following Buchan's advice, Mary Anne contacted John Dixon, a copper-plate printer, and began working out the details for a book of her brother's etchings. It was finally published in 1808, under the title *A Series of Etchings by James*

*complaining

Barry, Esq. From his Original and Justly Celebrated Paintings in The Great Room, etc. The Great Room was the display centre for artists in the Society of Arts, Manufactures and Commerce, and prints from a series of six of James' murals had been displayed there. These and other etchings were featured in the book, which carried a price tag of five guineas.

While Mary Anne was looking after the sale of James' paintings and art supplies and working through the final details of the book, Margaret found little to do. Time hung heavily on her hands.

"Mam, General Miranda said I could use his library if I liked. Would you be needing me this afternoon?"

Mary Anne smiled at her daughter. "I should have known you'd be puttin' your nose in a book before too long. Run along then. But mind your manners!"

General Miranda's library was grander than anything Margaret had ever dreamed of. He had more books than she had ever seen in one place. There were books about everything she could imagine. Books about travel. Books about government. Book after book on wars and battles. More books on politics. The books were in many languages, including Spanish, French, English and Latin.

Now she began her studies in earnest. As she read each book she thought carefully about what she was reading, storing some things in her memory, discarding others. She skimmed through some books. Others she pored over carefully, studying each page and reading aloud to herself. This time she paid attention to how she pronounced the words as well as to what they said.

Since her talk with the general, she had been listening to Londoners and noticed they spoke louder than the Irish. And where Irish sentences rose and fell with a musical cadence, English sentences seemed to come in short, flat bursts of sound. The Irish often dropped the final syllable of a word, turning *-ing* into *-in'*, but English people changed their words in different ways. Most often they seemed to do something odd with the beginnings of words. Sometimes they dropped letters, like the *h* in *home* and *horses,* turning them into *'ome* and *'orses.* At other times they added letters to the end of a word, especially words that ended in vowels. A girl named Sara might be called Sar-er. It was very confusing. The more closely Margaret listened to the English around her, the more she realized how many different dialects people spoke.

In general, though, she decided the English spoke more abruptly than the Irish. They always sounded as though there was somethin' a-botherin' them. Someth*ing* bother*ing* them, she corrected herself.

At times she thought about what she was doing and wondered just how quickly a person could lose one accent and learn another. "I wonder how long it would take before I could rent a room from one of the landladies who turned Mam down for being Irish," she mused.

At times she felt the sudden pangs of homesickness and wondered if she would ever see Ireland again. The countryside around Cork was so beautiful, all green and rolling. And the air was fresh and clean, spiced with the tang of the salt sea, not choking with soot and smoke as it was here in London. Cork was peaceful as well, not like London, whose sky was shattered by never-ending sounds: the rumble of iron cartwheels against stone roads, the shouts of tradesmen hawking their wares up and down the streets, the shouts and cries of children playing in the streets, yapping dogs, braying donkeys, neighing horses, the constant sound of people and, on rainy days (of which there seemed to be many), the clip-clop of pattens against the cobbles. Pattens were like sandals with iron or wooden soles. They were held on by leather straps and worn over the soft leather slippers used by men and women. The landlady loaned Margaret a pair of pattens one rainy day, but they were hard to wear.

She found them slippery against the uneven stones and had to keep re-adjusting the straps lest she slip and twist an ankle.

Often the girl paused during her reading to gently massage her temple. Things had turned out so different from what she had expected. Her family was scattered. Redmond had disappeared. No one knew where Patrick was. Her brother John had turned his back on them. They'd gone from a comfortable living in Cork to the brink of the poorhouse almost overnight. She shuddered to think how close they had come to being paupers. And as if that weren't bad enough, her mother had begun a frightening and shocking discussion.

"I think it's time to draw up a will," she told Margaret.

"Mam, you don't have to worry about that! You'll be here for years and years."

Mary Anne shook her head. "No, darlin', I'm thinkin' the palsy is gettin' worse. It's gettin' that much harder for me every day, and I feel wearier than I should."

Her concerns made Margaret realize that it was time to give serious thought to her future. She wanted to travel and see the world like her brother and her uncles had done. But that took money—substantial amounts of it. She had no prospects of marriage and didn't want to spend her life in domestic service working in some other woman's scullery or caring for another woman's children. It was difficult enough for a young girl to support herself and almost impossible to make enough money to do the things she wanted.

Sometime during this troubled period of her life she first considered the notion of an independent career. It couldn't be done as a woman. Women didn't have careers. At least not in London. Nor in Cork.

General Miranda had given her the idea of masquerading as a Londoner. But the Earl of Buchan and the general offered her another dream as well. Buchan believed in female education. In Europe, at the time, this was an outrageous notion. But Buchan persisted. Between 1791 and 1793 he had written a series of essays on the topic that were published in *The Bee* under the pen name Sophia. "Sophia" made a stinging comparison between European attitudes towards woman and the Chinese custom of crushing the feet of women with tight bindings to achieve a standard of beauty while ignoring that the practice crippled women for life.

"The men of Europe have crushed the heads of women in their infancy, and then laughed at them because their brains are not so well formed," Sophia wrote, referring not to the physical crushing of heads but the crushing of minds and the stunting of mental abilities.

Buchan and his wife had no children although he had one natural son, whose education was ensured. In Margaret, Buchan found himself faced with both a challenge and an opportunity. Here was a young woman crying out for education—an education that would be wasted. The best she could hope for was to make a good marriage. In return for financial security she would be faced with the prospect of, in Sophia's words, "attachment to splendor of dress, excessive curiosity to discover secrets and excessive desire of prying into the trifling business of our acquaintances, of public shows of all kinds in our youth and attachments to card-playing in our old age." It was not an exciting prospect.

"Women deserve an education," Buchan said.

Miranda agreed. Like Buchan he was appalled by the waste of female intelligence, but he equated it to a larger theme. Political freedom was essential for the well-being of a nation. Freedom from artificial restrictions of gender were equally important for the well-being of women. As Buchan and Miranda mused over Margaret's situation, they realized the possibility that stood before them. Margaret had almost no one in the world, save only a very ill mother. There was no family to interfere. She had no attachments in London, was virtually unknown and had no remaining contacts in Ireland. It would be relatively easy for her to keep a secret.

"If you were trained in something—like medicine—there might be a place for you in Venezuela," Miranda told her.

"Venezuela?" she breathed.

"Yes, Venezuela," Miranda smiled. "We could share our dreams, my little Margarita."

Miranda often called her that. The name meant "Daisy" and she liked the affectionate way he said it. His manner was kindly, almost like a grandfather's.

Margaret knew the dream to which he referred. He hoped one day to free his homeland by leading an army to Venezuela to overthrow Spain and the oppressive Spanish rule that gripped his country. Once that was done he would become the dictator of Venezuela. Dictator meant absolute ruler. From that position he could guide the country to a free and democratic form of government.

"You could be my personal physician," he told her.

Margaret looked at him blankly.

"Yes," he nodded, "I think you could learn to become a doctor."

"But . . . but women can't be doctors," she sputtered.

"And why not?" he asked.

"Why, because they just can't. Everyone knows that. There's never been a—I don't even know what you could call it. Doctoress?"

Miranda laughed. "Not doctoress, Margarita. Just doctor. And there has already been one."

"There has?"

"In Germany a young woman named Dorothea Leporin-Erxleben became a doctor. It was many years ago, before you were born, but she and her brother studied with their father, who was a physician in Quedlinburg. The University of Halle in Germany awarded her a degree. But they accepted no other women after her."

Margaret shook her head. "I've never even heard of her."

Buchan joined in. "Not many people have, but the fact is women can be doctors just like men if they have the same training."

"You could do it, Margarita," the general repeated. "But first you must prepare yourself for admission to a medical school."

"And you would have to study hard enough to pass each of the courses," Buchan added.

It was a staggering idea. Was it truly possible? Could she do it? Medicine was difficult. There was so much to learn: drugs, chemicals, potions and compounds. There were many things that would not be easy to face. Along with their studies doctors had to contend with the pain and suffering of their patients—the sick, dying and desperate who fell under their care. What might it feel like to operate on a living human being? Could she make herself wield a scalpel and cut into warm living flesh? How would she cope with the infection and putrid smells that went with some diseases? Being a doctor was surely much harder than being a midwife or an herbal woman. Birth was natural and midwifery did not require cutting. Herbal healers dealt with potions of teas, salves and ointments. They might even be pleasant lines of work, she thought.

And yet the notion of medicine appealed to her. If she could learn enough to ease her mother's palsy, that would be a blessing.

Now her mind turned to more practical things.

"But how could I do it?" she asked. "Women can't go to medical schools."

She couldn't even remember which of her mentors spoke the next words.

"You could if they thought you were a man."

The sentence echoed in her mind: . . . *If they thought you were a man.*

Pretending to be a man would be much harder than pretending to be a Londoner. But if that was what it took to enter medical school, Margaret decided she was prepared to try. In any case, as the general had said, it was only until she graduated. By that time he would be in Venezuela and she could join him there.

"In my free country we will celebrate the independence of women along with the independence of the nation. You will lead the way for other women."

Over the next few weeks she began an unofficial course of study. This time, along with listening to people, she watched them. She looked at men, watched their mannerisms, then practised when she got home. How did they walk? How did they sit? What did they do? How did they greet each other? What did they talk about among themselves?

Learning how to behave like a man was not easy. Men did not sit with their knees together and their ankles crossed demurely. Men did not pat at their hair or fuss with their clothing. Men did not stand back and wait for someone else to make decisions. Nor did they hurry to serve each other bowls of tea or dishes of sweets. Men waited for someone to serve them or simply took what they wanted.

"I'll never be able to fool anyone," Margaret groaned as she found herself making one silly mistake after another. There was so much to learn. Her whole world had turned upside down and inside out.

Gradually, though, she became more convincing in her role. Her temper, always on a short fuse, was sorely tested during these weeks, but in time she began to have more confidence in herself and her ability to carry out the masquerade.

She was ready for the next step.

Chapter Three

MIRANDA AND BUCHAN

MARGARET SPENT many pleasant hours in General Miranda's wonderful library. There were books of all sorts for her to explore in many different languages. Like many Irish people at the time, Margaret was familiar with several languages. She knew English, had studied Latin in the convent school and had learned some classical Greek, with its oddly shaped letters, in the hedge schools. And even though the Irish were forbidden to speak or write Gaelic, she loved the beautiful Celtic letters of her native language and the musical sounds of the words.

Margaret found that what she had learned in the hedge schools and from the Sisters at the convent gave her a good grounding. The hedge schools, where students learned Greek and other subjects, were illegal under the hated penal laws. They were held in the shelter of the hedges and taught by travelling teachers who were often well-educated priests forced out of their parishes by the English. Children in Irish villages gathered in safe concealment beside the hedges and eagerly learned all they could from the teacher before he travelled on to the next village. It was too dangerous for teachers to stay in one place for long, so every minute in the school was precious.

Now, with a little help, Margaret was able to read Miranda's books in Latin and Greek. Not all of them, and not easily, but enough that she could figure out their contents. She knew that with practice she would get better.

"You'll have to concentrate on Latin," Buchan told her. "Church Latin isn't enough. Your examinations will be given in that language, and as a doctor, you'll need to be proficient in it."

"Why do doctors use Latin?" she asked.

"It's the mother of all languages," Buchan replied. "It's the language of educated people as well. If you speak Latin you can easily understand French and Spanish. And of course, because doctors everywhere speak Latin, you can speak with them anywhere in the civilized world, no matter what their country."

Margaret nodded.

"I have many things to do in the next while," Miranda told her, "so I won't be here all the time to help you, but I'll keep a place for you in free Venezuela."

"Venezuela," she repeated. "It's such a beautiful name. And from what you tell me, the country is as beautiful as its name. I can hardly wait to see it."

The two men were pleased with the progress she'd made in losing her Irish accent. "It's still there," Buchan said, "but it's very faint. I think you will be able to pass yourself off as a Londoner fairly soon."

Once again Margaret turned to her studies, now advancing to more difficult work. Sometimes her brain buzzed with the amount of information she was trying to pack into it. There was so much, and she had so little time. But the more she studied, the more she read and the more she learned, the more interesting the work became. Soon she found herself looking forward to her assignments and seeking extra information when something in a text puzzled her.

Time flew by, but when the Earl of Buchan announced that he would arrange for her to be admitted to the University of Edinburgh in the fall, Margaret's heart raced. "So soon?" she asked.

"You'll be fine. It's recognized as the best medical school in the land. But we must have a new name for you. Your present one simply won't do."

Margaret had giggled at the thought of calling herself Mr. Margaret. She had thought from time to time about a suitable name, something that would match her new persona. She rejected her father's name, Jeremiah Bulkley, her brother's name, John Bulkley, and her grandfather's name, John Barry. Briefly she considered taking Daniel Reardon's name but turned that down, too. She wanted to retain some links with her family, but not make them obvious to anyone but her.

When she eventually chose a name, it had an elegant sound. She whispered it to herself many times, enjoying its complex rhythms. Now, for the first time, she said the name out loud.

"I would like to honour my family," she told the Earl, "and I want to honour both of you as well, for all you have done for me. With your permission I will call myself James Miranda Stuart Barry, and soon I shall be known as Doctor James Barry."

Buchan smiled, pleased by the compliment she had given him.

"And now the play begins," said Buchan. "We shall see, my dear, just how capable an actress you are."

❧❧❧

Upstairs in one of the bedrooms at General Miranda's, the slender red-headed girl peered anxiously into the cheval glass, a long mirror mounted on a frame. Margaret laughed to herself as she pulled on a pair of men's trousers for the first time. "What a lot of bothersome flaps and buttons," she said as she wriggled and squirmed into them. "I'm thinking that skirts are a lot more comfortable. Still," she mused, attempting to make the pants sit comfortably on her slim hips, "I won't miss having to tie up all those petticoat strings."

The trousers were too long and flapped around the middle of her shins like the clothes on a scarecrow. "It looks like I've borrowed my brother John's clothing," she giggled. Pantaloons were meant to tie neatly below the knee, but these kept sliding down her leg and dragging her long stockings with them. Sighing, she pulled off the pantaloons and began again, gartering the stockings more tightly this time, then fastening the strings of the pantaloons snugly to prevent them from shifting out of place.

Once the pantaloons were secured, she reached for the long-sleeved shirt and pulled it on over her head. Her fingers fumbled awkwardly with the neck buttons. "Oh, of course!" She smiled at her forgetfulness. "The buttons are all on backwards." That was something else she'd have to get used to. Like most women, Margaret was accustomed to buttoning the right side of her clothing over the left side. Now she would have to remember that men's clothing buttoned in the opposite direction with the left side over the right.

"I wonder why things button up differently on men's clothing than on women's clothing?" she mused. Some people said it was because women were dressed by their maids, so the buttons were put on for the convenience of the maids. Some women were indeed dressed by their maids, but certainly more women dressed themselves. And men were often dressed by their valets, so their buttons should be reversed as well. It was a puzzle.

"Oh, well. Never mind the why of it. I'll just have to remember that that's the way it is," she scolded herself.

The shirt was obviously made for someone with much wider shoulders than Margaret's, and the sleeves hung down well below her fingertips. Laughing, she flapped her arms at her reflection in the mirror. Once the sleeves were shortened and the cuffs were tied up, it wouldn't be too bad, she supposed.

The next item perplexed her. It was a tie-like stock that

men wore around their necks. She'd watched her mam tie on her da's and her brother John's stocks, but she'd never done it herself. Grimly she stepped closer to the mirror and began twisting the cloth into place. The fabric was lightweight, over six feet in length. First she folded it lengthwise in half. Then she began wrapping it about her slender neck. Two wraps around the neck left her with ends that dangled well below her waist. Three wraps was just right. Then she discovered the ends were uneven, and she had to begin all over again. Once it was wrapped smoothly, she looped one end under the other and smoothed the two ends down her front.

Some men, she knew, wore a large brooch to hold the ends in place. Others, the "dandies" who dressed in a more fanciful manner, looped the ends of the stock into a wide bow. Margaret decided to stay with the more conventional wrap.

Carefully she tucked the long ends of the shirt into the top of her pantaloons, then pulled on a brocaded vest that hung well below the waist. She buttoned the vest, then tucked the longest of the stock ends into her waistcoat. Only then did she turn again towards the mirror, this time looking critically at her reflection, trying to see herself through a stranger's eyes.

"I wish there was some way to add to my stature," she murmured. She drew herself up to her full height of almost five feet, even flexing her ankles to raise herself up a fraction of an inch more. But it didn't help.

"I'll just have to remember to stand up straight at all times. That's what the sisters at the convent always told us to do, and that's why they had such lovely posture. They looked like queens in their long flowing robes."

Margaret continued her scrutiny of her reflection. The disguise just might pass, but there was one serious problem. No matter what she wore, her hair was a complete give-away.

"Well, there's no other way, I suppose," she told herself, reaching for a sharp pair of sewing scissors in the wicker basket on a nearby table. "Men just don't wear their hair in long loops and curls."

Taking a deep breath, she grabbed a handful of her long thick hair and held it tightly just above shoulder level. Swiftly she opened the scissors and began savagely cutting through the first handful of bright red strands.

The job was quickly completed. Margaret looked in shock at her reflection. Quickly averting her eyes, she looked at the floor. The sight of her beautiful hair lying there in careless piles was devastating.

Quickly she grabbed a hairbrush and stroked the hair towards the back of her neck, pulling it together neatly as she tied it with a strip of narrow black grosgrain ribbon.

"There. That's doesn't look too bad," she told herself. "Well," she amended, peering closely into the mirror, "at least it doesn't look very womanly."

She turned away from the mirror and gathered up the piles of hair, thrusting them out of sight in a nearby leather wastebasket. She picked up a pair of soft black slippers and fitted them onto her feet. The slippers were a little wide, but that could be fixed with a few stitches. A pair of pattens stood nearby. She would need them if she went outside, but no one wore them indoors.

Once again she faced the mirror. A stranger looked back at her—someone who might have been related, but certainly not the young girl she usually saw. A sudden thought struck her and she began to giggle. "If only my Grannie Barry could see me now!" John and Juliana Barry, her mother's parents, had been so pleased when Margaret was born.

"They always wanted a granddaughter," her mother had often told her. "They had four boys before I was born, but I was the only girl. None of my brothers married, and I remember me mam greetin'* about whether they'd ever have any grandchildren. They were that happy when me and your da got married. When your brother, John, was born they loved him, of course, but when you arrived you just stole their hearts away."

Grannie and Granddad were long dead now. They'd died when Margaret was a young girl, but she could still remember the warm hugs, the funny games and the silly songs they'd shared. What would they say if they could see their only granddaughter now?

With a last look at herself, she turned and ran out of the room, skimming down the staircase to the drawing room below, where her two friends were waiting.

"Well, sirs! What do you think?" she demanded, pirouetting before them with her arms outstretched.

"I think the first thing you must do is stop dancing about on your toes," said General Francisco de Miranda, trying to hide a smile. "That is very much out of character for a gentleman."

"Indeed it is," the second man agreed. David Stuart Erskine, the eleventh Earl of Buchan, was to be a powerful ally to the young girl, and without his support the plan dreamed up by General Miranda could never be put into action. Buchan had used his influence to help Margaret enter a university, and he would later introduce her to friends who could be of assistance during her studies and later still to friends who could help her in her career.

"I'm sure you'll learn quickly," he told her. "It will just be difficult at the beginning."

Now the two men looked at each other. Could Margaret carry out the plan they had made for her? Could she successfully impersonate a young man, or, as had happened in so many other instances, would she be found out? More importantly, could she catch up with the young men who had

* *fussing*

enjoyed a regular education and hold her own with them in the classroom and in the operating theatre? That would be the more difficult challenge and the most important. Margaret could not have the luxury of merely passing her courses. She must do well in each and every one—well enough to withstand the challenges that were bound to come.

Each man weighed the prospect in his mind.

"I think she'll do," said Miranda.

"I agree," replied Buchan.

Now Buchan turned to an older woman, who sat on a chair near the door.

"What do you think, Mrs. Bulkley?" he asked.

"'Tis astonished I am, sir," she replied. "I didn't know she was goin' to be cuttin' off all that beautiful hair."

"It's all right, Mam," Margaret replied, addressing her mother fondly. "It's all right," she repeated. *"Níl buartha.** My hair will grow back before you can blink. And I can wear a bonnet in the meantime."

"But why would you do that?" Miranda interrupted. "If you are going to be a man, you must be one for twenty-four hours a day. You cannot expect to switch back and forth. It would be far too difficult for you."

Shocked, Margaret could only look at him. She had not thought of that. Somehow she assumed she could go to school dressed in men's clothing, then revert to being a girl when she came home. But of course Miranda was right. Dressing as a girl would only add to the danger that she might be discovered.

Buchan smiled at the young woman.

"It seems hard now," he said, "but I'm sure you'll soon get the hang of it. And once you've finished school and are safely in Venezuela with the general, why, you can be anything you want!"

*Don't be worried.

Giving the young woman a moment to compose herself, the earl turned to Margaret's mother. "She'll do splendidly, Mrs. Bulkley," he said, his clear blue eyes peering at her from under the shaggy eyebrows that marked the Buchan men. "Now perhaps you can talk to the sewing woman and see about something that fits a little better. I'm not sure if you can have those clothes altered to fit, but in any case she'll need several sets of clothing. Do you need a list of some sort or do you know what to get?"

For the first time the older woman smiled. "No trouble with that, m'lord," she said. "Between me brothers, me husband and me son, I've seen to the clothing of many men."

Ruefully she shook her head, then stretched out her shaking hands. "I'd be doin' it myself this time, too, but these hands can't handle fine work like sewing anymore. Still, I'm sure the general's housekeeper, Mrs. Martin, can give me the name of a sewing woman."

It had taken awhile to sort out the confusion over Miranda's housekeeper. The general referred to her by her true name, Sara Abraham, but the woman, who was the mother of Miranda's son, preferred to call herself Mrs. George Martin, the name Miranda had used during part of his time in America. Gradually Mrs. Martin became accustomed to Margaret's presence in the general's house and in time the two had become friendly.

Now Mary Anne beckoned to Margaret, who followed her out through the wide doorway and into the hall. "You can take off that clothin' and I'll find Mrs. Martin," Mary Anne murmured.

The two men watched as the women climbed the stairs, Margaret skipping along lithely, her mother moving more slowly. Miranda and Buchan were an unlikely pair. One was a native of Venezuela, born to a Venezuelan mother and a Spanish father. The other was a Scottish nobleman. At first glance they seemed to have nothing in common, but in fact deeply shared beliefs and causes bound them together.

❧❧❧

Francisco de Miranda was a remarkable man. His father, Sebastian de Miranda, emigrated from the Canary Islands to South America, where he became a successful linen merchant in Caracas. There he met and married Francisca Antonia Rodriguez Espinosa.

Their first child, born in Caracas on March 28, 1750, was baptized Sebastian Francisco. The boy went to the Academy of Santa Rosa and the University of Caracas. In January 1771 he was given permission to leave Venezuela and sailed from La Guaira to Cadiz to enter the service of the king of Spain.

In Madrid he made a slight change to his name, signing himself "Francisco Sebastian" instead of "Sebastian Francisco." Soon after, he omitted "Sebastian" entirely. In December 1772, Francisco de Miranda bought a commission as captain in the Princess Infantry Regiment for eight thousand pesos. In 1774–75 his regiment was assigned to serve in a campaign against the Muslims of Morocco and Algiers.

It was not long, however, before Miranda became bored with the routine duties to which he was assigned. His commission was not what he'd expected, nor had he anticipated serving under a cranky despot like Juan de Roca, the colonel of the regiment. The two quarreled incessantly. Miranda tried to transfer out of the Princess Regiment, but his attempts were frustrated until the beginning of the American Revolution. At that time a secret treaty between France and Spain brought the Spanish into battle on the side of America's thirteen colonies, which were at war against the British.

Miranda was assigned to General Juan Manuel de Cagigal, the governor of Cuba. Under Cagigal, Miranda served in the siege of Pensacola, the capital of East Florida. The British garrison at Pensacola was defeated early in May 1781. Miranda's performance earned him a promotion to colonel.

Miranda next saw action in an attack on New Providence, the capital of the Bahama Islands, then held by Britain. The garrison surrendered on May 8, 1782, ceding the Bahamas to Spain.

During his eight years of service, Miranda rose rapidly but left in his wake many jealousies. His enemies made a number of charges, and Miranda was arrested. He was sent to Cuba to be tried in Havana. One of the charges against Miranda was that he was fond of the English, which was true, but he admired the Americans as well. The American Revolution had made a great impression on him, and he dreamed of liberating South America from Spanish rule.

The court in Cuba found Miranda guilty, stripped him of his commission, levied a fine and sentenced him to ten years in prison. Several years later the Council of the Indies exonerated him completely. At the time, however, Miranda believed the court was prejudiced against him, so he decided his best move was to flee its jurisdiction. Escaping from Cuba, he travelled to America and spent most of eighteen months on the eastern seaboard under the assumed name of George Martin. Then he travelled to Holland, the Crimea, Greece and the Russian border before recrossing Europe and arriving in England in June 1789.

Once settled in London, he began lobbying the British prime minister, William Pitt, for England's help in freeing the Spanish Indies. Pitt declined. The Nootka Treaty had just been signed, ending a dispute between England and Spain that centred on the west coast of what later became known as Canada. Trouble had begun when a Spanish captain, Esteban Martinez, seized Captain James Culnett and the entire crew of the British ships *Argonaut* and *Princess Royal*. They had been on their way to Nootka Sound, on the west coast of Vancouver Island, to establish a trading post.

Spain had laid claim to the land and accused Culnett of trespassing. The Nootka dispute was the first international case heard at the World Court at The Hague. After lengthy debates the court arrived at a decision on January 11, 1794. Spain remained in control of her American colonies, and Nootka was declared a free port. Spain had to compensate England for the loss of the two ships.

By the time Miranda arrived in London, Pitt had no wish to antagonize the powerful nation that was now an ally. Discouraged, Miranda decided to offer his services to France, where the French Revolution had just erupted. He was accepted and given the rank of general. In 1798 he returned to England, once again lobbying Pitt for support for his revolutionary projects. Once again Pitt declined.

For a time Miranda turned attention to his collection of documents. He had started it in 1771, when he left Venezuela, with a collection of documents about his family. Gradually the collection expanded to include copies of other important manuscripts, maps, papers and plans concerning the Spanish colonies in America. His habit of saving letters continued, and now he added copies of his outgoing correspondence as well. Many of these letters were to and from persons of historical importance. This information, along with pamphlets and other material, became part of a series of more than sixty volumes, which Miranda added to throughout his life. It became an exhaustive and impressive information resource. In time the entire collection came into the possession of Henry, the third Earl of Bathurst, who stored it carefully.

During Miranda's years in London, he had a personal library of over six thousand volumes. At the time it was one of the largest and best private libraries in London and, it is believed, in all of England as well.

This was the library he opened to Margaret Bulkley. In a letter to him, she wrote, "Your library is a treasure which I value above all others. I can not begin to express my gratitude to you for allowing me to use it."

Miranda's interest in young minds was not limited to Margaret. While in London he founded the Lautaro Society, a group of young adults interested in issues of political freedom. The group was named for Lautaro, a chief of the Araucanian Indians in Mexico. Lautaro had fought bravely against the conquistadors when Spain seized the Mexican Empire. His name reminded the young people that while liberty did not come easily, with hard work it was possible. Miranda also is reported to have been a member of the Logia Lautaro, a Masonic group.

In his own way, David Stuart Erskine was an equally remarkable person. He shared Miranda's passion for liberty, but not in far-off exotic places. One of Buchan's dreams was to bring political freedom to Scotland, where elections were controlled by the English.

Buchan's reverence for his Scottish homeland was shown in many ways. Perhaps one of the most touching was his presentation of a gift to American president George Washington in 1792. One of Scotland's best-loved heroes was William Wallace, who had led the Scottish resistance movement protesting Edward I's takeover in 1296. Wallace had spearheaded battles at Stirling Bridge in 1297 and at Falkirk in 1298. Folklore had it that, when wounded, he rested under a tree, then rose and continued the battle. One of Buchan's protégés, the Scottish poet Robert Burns, wrote of Wallace, commemorating the event with his famous lines, "I'll lay me doon and bleed awhile, then rise to fight again." In his *Bruce at Bannockburn,* Burns captured Wallace's spirit:

Scots, wha hae wi' Wallace bled
Scots, wham Bruce has aften led;
Welcome to your gory bed,
Or to glorious victorie!

Buchan's gift to George Washington evoked these images and history. It was a snuffbox made from the tree that had sheltered Wallace almost five hundred years earlier.

Buchan worked tirelessly towards his goal, using the best weapon at his disposal: his writing. He published countless essays and editorials in newspapers across the land. Some dismissed him as a crank, but others gave thoughtful consideration to what he said. Buchan believed freedom meant more than simple ownership of land or avoiding physical control by conquering armies. He believed passionately in freedom of the mind. And unlike most of his contemporaries, he believed the mind of a woman was just as important as the mind of a man.

Buchan's reason for believing in the capabilities of the female mind were very personal. He had received a large part of his early education from his mother, Agnes Stuart. She had studied mathematics under Colin Maclauarin and imparted to her young son not only a love of mathematics but also a standard against which he measured other women. Many, if not most, Englishmen of the day laughed at Buchan for a series of essays he published between 1791 and 1793. In each he made a strong case for educating females.

These articles drew many negative replies. Most writers pointed out that the "common traits of women" made it impossible to educate them. It was a widely held view among men that was shared, surprisingly, by many women.

Buchan continued, however, to publish essays. He noted that, among other things, the faults unfairly described as the "common traits of women" were in truth simply due to their lack of education. "These same faults are also common among uneducated men," he wrote. "It is sad that society wastes so many brilliant minds by choosing to 'finish' girls instead of giving them a proper education."

"Finishing" a girl meant sending her to a special school,

called a finishing school, where she learned such things as manners, social conventions and graces, including how to instruct servants in proper table settings, how to arrange flowers and how to make polite conversation.

Buchan firmly believed that girls *could* think and that a proper education would not be wasted on them. He found it difficult to convince his peers that girls were capable of learning anything more difficult than fancy embroidery, playing the harpsichord (an early form of piano) or singing harmonies with their friends.

In any case, most people believed women had enough to bother their heads about with managing the servants, who did the housework, and keeping up with social engagements. Women not fortunate enough to have servants were often too busy simply surviving to worry about what they might be able to learn in school. There were, however, a few women who did overcome incredible obstacles to make worthwhile contributions to society.

Two of Buchan's favourite books were written by Mary Wollstonecraft. The first, *Thoughts on the Education of Daughters,* was published in 1786. The second, *A Vindication of the Rights of Women,* was published in 1792. Buchan believed they should be required reading for all educators and all educated people. Wollstonecraft and Buchan were active correspondents and shared opinions on a number of topics. He was deeply saddened when, in 1797, she died just eleven days after the birth of her second daughter, who also bore the name Mary.

Buchan maintained a wide range of correspondents, including members of the royal family. He was a descendent of the Stuarts, the royal house of Scotland until its throne was occupied by the English, and claimed kinship with the royal family. They appear to have allowed and enjoyed that claim.

Buchan's interests covered a wide range of subjects. He

was a patron of the arts, but unlike many wealthy people of the day, he did not simply support "popular" artists and writers. Instead he encouraged those whose talent he genuinely enjoyed and often helped them to become popular. Buchan's support of Robert Burns, who was largely ignored outside his native Scotland, made him famous in England and on the continent of Europe as well. And, of course, he sponsored the Irish historical painter James Barry.

Buchan had a serious side, but he also was something of an eccentric and had a wild sense of humour. Society was often shocked by his pranks. One of his most outrageous involved a group of nine modest young society ladies from Edinburgh who were invited to join him at breakfast. As the story goes, they were to sit for a portrait of *Apollo and the Muses* with Buchan as Apollo and the young ladies as the Muses.

The women donned their costumes and gathered in the studio, where an artist was waiting. Then Cupid entered—a young man Buchan hired for the role. Cupid's entire costume consisted of a bow and arrow. Buchan roared with laughter as the young women ran screaming from the room.

The earl was a very wealthy man but in his younger days decided he didn't want to live an idle life. He wanted a meaningful career. He chose diplomacy and applied to the British government for a diplomatic post. The government offered him the post of under-secretary to their Spanish legation. The idea amused him, and he was on the verge of accepting when he realized he was socially superior to the man in charge of the legation. It simply wouldn't do to work for someone lower on the social scale than he! That ended his diplomatic career.

Buchan might not have completely embraced the notion of democracy, but he did recognize individual values, and many of his causes had both weight and significance. One of his most commendable attributes was his compassion. He knew how to assist others without belittling them. Margaret's uncle, James Barry, was a good case in point. Even when most others had turned their backs on Barry, Buchan continued to offer his support. After Barry's death he continued this support, assisting both Margaret and her mother. It was typical of the man who, rather than simply settling a pension on Margaret, sponsored her admission to a university and arranged what help he could without offending her pride or making her feel subservient.

Whether he intended to help Margaret reveal herself as a woman after her graduation is not known. It would have been the ultimate joke on a society that scorned the learning abilities of women. Perhaps the denouement would have come when she was safely in Venezuela under Miranda's care and protection. Miranda and Buchan had very different motives, but Margaret was valuable to both of them.

Now it was up to Margaret to prove, or disprove, their theories.

Chapter Four

EDINBURGH

L IFE AT 6 LOTHIAN STREET in Edinburgh was more exciting now but also more difficult than either Margaret or her mother had imagined. It was hard for Mary Anne to remember to call her daughter James and equally hard for Margaret not to call her mother Mam. At first she called her Aunt when they were with other people. Then she realized it might seem unusual for a student from London to have an aunt from Ireland. And it could be a clue to her identity. Quickly she made up her mind. Rather than Aunt, Mary Anne would be introduced as her housekeeper and called Mrs. Bulkley. It was difficult at first. Not only did it seem strange and formal to Margaret, but it was hard for her mother as well. Each time Margaret called her Mrs. Bulkley, her mother looked up in surprise as though expecting someone else to be speaking.

"I know, I know. Ye have to do it, but 'tis *doiligh** for me to listen to me own wee girl speakin' to me like a stranger." Quickly she added, "Now, now. Don't get yourself all upset. I'll not forget. But if I should, don't be angry." To herself she added, "Even if I live to be a hundred and two, 'twill never sound right."

Margaret continued to struggle with her English accent, but each day she sounded more like the Londoner she claimed to be. Each day, too, she felt more like the young man

*difficult

she appeared to be. As she grew more accustomed to masculine clothing, she found less need to fuss and fidget with it. She did make a few changes, though, to help with her disguise. She took her boots to a neighbourhood cobbler. For a few pennies he raised them up, adding extra soles and heels, to make her appear a little taller.

She also gave careful thought to the traditional short jacket worn by other students. "What do you think, Mrs. Bulkley?" she asked, modelling a jacket in front of her mother.

"If you're looking for an honest answer, 'tis nothin' that will help your disguise," Mary Anne replied.

Looking into the mirror, Margaret nodded. Her mother was right. The jacket only called attention to her rounded hips and narrow waist. Instead she bought a full-length coat, which she wore to class every day. Along with concealing her waist and hips, the coat made her look a little sturdier.

Her most difficult challenge was making herself appear older. Unlike her fellow students, she had no trace of a beard or mustache on her face, and her complexion was smooth and pale. Her voice was softer and higher than the voices of the young men in her class, and her hands were small and delicate. She also had a small stature, slight build and undeveloped muscles. Margaret knew she could never convince anyone she was the same age as her classmates, most of whom were between eighteen and twenty.

Since she couldn't change her appearance to match her age, she changed her age to match her appearance. In both the University of Edinburgh records and the Home Office medical enlistment forms, James Barry's date of birth is entered as 1795. If this were her true birth date, Margaret would have been something of a child prodigy. She was probably closer to twenty and may have been older. But it served her purpose well to be thought of as much younger. She looked more like a fourteen year old boy than someone in his late teens or early twenties.

Her classmates accepted her story. Her high marks and classroom performance made it easy to believe that she was, indeed, a prodigy. Many university students of the day thoroughly enjoyed their careers as scholars but did not let their studies interfere with their pleasures. Margaret was different. She applied herself diligently to her course work, completing each of the required assignments and doing extra work as well. She attended all the lectures and took her own notes. Some less serious students simply bought their notes, and if they attended lectures they paid little attention to the lecturer. In their eyes, Margaret's attitude confirmed her status as a prodigy, and she quickly won the regard of both students and teachers.

There was another advantage to pretending to be so young: the other students did not expect her to take part in the drinking and partying that many of them enjoyed. That was particularly good given the dragon of a housekeeper who hovered in the background and kept a watchful eye on any goings-on involving their young classmate.

Several of Margaret's fellow students became quite protective of her and recognized that she had very special abilities. At times they felt the flare of her temper, but on the whole they enjoyed her company.

If classroom studies were sometimes boring, the practical parts of the course were not. Under supervision, students practised on real patients, most of whom were unable to afford regular doctors. In return for accepting the care of students, patients paid greatly reduced fees or in some cases no fees at all. The patients came from the poorest sections of Edinburgh. The crowded rooms they lived in created perfect conditions for the spread of contagious diseases. Their bodies, weakened by poor nutrition and unhealthy living, showed signs of degenerative diseases as well. On clinic days they sat in long listless lines outside the university doors, hoping they would be lucky enough to be treated.

At times the student doctors responded to emergency calls and had to seek out their patients in the city's crowded tenement districts. Robbery, theft, muggings and assaults were common. The young doctors were targets of crime as well. Instructors regularly warned their students, "Be on guard when you go into the tenements. Felons are apt to attack when you least expect it. They'll steal your medical bags and sell them for whatever they can get. They have no regard for human life. Be cautious about asking for directions. That marks you as an outsider and makes you fair prey."

Margaret enjoyed the challenge of these emergency cases. They were an exciting change from the chronic diseases that plagued most clinic patients, but she was nervous about travelling through the rougher parts of Edinburgh.

"Look here, Barry," said one of her classmates, a young man named Jobson, "this simply won't do. You can't continue creeping and cringing about like a woman. When you're accosted by a tough, stand up to him. Look him in the eye and make him move off. If that doesn't work, a sharp jab with your fist will do the trick."

"Couldn't I just slap him?" she asked.

Jobson hooted with laughter. "Come off it. You'll never frighten anyone away with a slap. Just double up your fist and give him a good punch, just like you do when you're sparring."

Margaret drew a quick breath. "Jobson, I've never punched anyone with my fist."

"You're joking me," he replied.

"No, I'm not."

"Didn't your father teach you to box? Or your tutor?"

She shook her head. "No. My father died when I was very young. I'm sure he would have taught me to box, but he never had the chance."

The young man thought for a moment.

"Well, that's easily remedied. Take off your shirt and I'll

teach you something about the manly art of boxing."

Margaret removed her jacket but flatly refused to take off her shirt.

Jobson patiently explained the basics of boxing to her.

"Double up your fist," he instructed.

Margaret obediently screwed up her hand, tucking her thumb tightly inside her palm.

"No, no, no, Barry," Jobson howled. "That's an invitation to a broken thumb. Keep the thumb outside. Now make a hard fist. Harder. You have to hit someone with that, not give them a love poke."

Try as she would she could not block, counter or deliver a blow.

"I'm sorry," she apologized. "Let me try again."

The next round ended the same way with Margaret in tears.

"Confound it, Barry," Jobson shouted. "When I give you a punch in the ribs, you can't just cross your arms over your chest and duck away. You have to punch back!"

"But it hurts!" Margaret wailed.

"Of course it hurts. That's the whole idea of it. What do you think one of those toughs is going to do, tickle you? Now stand up and fight like a man."

Eventually Jobson gave up trying to teach her to box.

"It's probably just as well if you don't learn to fight," he told her. "You're only going to get hurt. It would be better if you simply learned to keep out of trouble."

"I'm afraid of breaking my hand," Margaret replied. "That could put an end to surgery for me."

Jobson nodded. "I don't understand why you want to be a surgeon. Being a doctor is good enough for me. Let someone else do the cutting and hacking."

"It's not cutting and hacking," Margaret snapped and then blushed as she realized Jobson was teasing her.

"Look, Barry. Most of us make sure we travel in groups of two or three when we go down into the tenements. I'll go with you if you like, and I know a couple of my friends will come as well."

"I can't wake you up in the middle of the night for a call," she protested.

"Yes, you can," Jobson said. "I'd rather go with you than stay behind and worry about you."

"I'll do the same for you," she promised, but Jobson only laughed at her offer.

"I appreciate the thought, but I'd be far happier if you'd spend some time with me swotting for exams. You pick up every word the instructor says. I don't know how you remember things the way you do, but I wouldn't mind at all if you'd spend a little time going over it with me."

"Done," she cried, and both laughed as they shook hands on the deal.

Margaret loved the long hours she spent each day in class, and each evening she brought home more work to do.

"My hands are full of wonderful things," she wrote in a letter to Buchan. "I work from about seven each morning until two the next morning—and still I look for more."

Each day Margaret learned new information and new techniques to meet new challenges. She was an exceptional student and consistently led the class. It wasn't long before her professors recognized her ability. To her delight she was given the job of dresser, applying and removing bandages.

"It's wonderful," she told her mother. "I'm working right beside the instructors at the demonstration table and don't have to jostle for a position with everyone else. I can see clearly everything they do!"

While Margaret was enjoying her adventure, Mrs. Bulkley was not finding life so pleasant. Repeatedly Mary Anne asked her daughter to take time from her studies to write letters to

Daniel Reardon. Mary Anne's palsy was now so bad she could hardly shape the letters of her name for the signature that she carefully added to the letters Margaret wrote. Each letter seemed to say the same thing. Daniel had to send them more money.

He sent it, but grudgingly. Each time they received a letter from him it repeated the same message: they couldn't continue to spend money at their present rate. There was wasn't enough income to cover it.

James Barry's large paintings had finally been sold, but Mary Anne had left behind most of the five hundred sets of books printed by John Dixon with instructions that her cousin was to sell them and send her the proceeds. Reardon tried his best to find customers, but there wasn't much interest in books of etchings.

But Mary Anne wouldn't give up. She was convinced the books would sell if Daniel would only try a little harder. Letter after letter contained suggestions for increasing sales. "I see that trade with America has resumed," she dictated as Margaret carefully wrote down the words. "Can you sell some of the books there?"

At other times she questioned her cousin about selling her parents' home in Cork. "I feel sure it could be sold for a good return," she told Margaret. "Write that down. Let Daniel know that I expect him to do somethin' about it. Tell him I want him to look after it as soon as possible and to send me the money quickly."

In August 1809 Mary Anne finally saw an attorney and drew up her will. Her husband, Jeremiah, was not mentioned. Her son, John, got nothing. Her brothers, Patrick and Redmond, were not named. Two mourning rings were to go to her cousin and his wife, formally named in the will as Mr. and Mrs. Reardon of Corbet Court in London, and another pair of mourning rings to Mr. and Mrs. R. Bonomi. Mourning rings and brooches, popular at that time, contained a lock of hair from the deceased. Everything else was for Margaret.

A few weeks later, Daniel informed her that her brother, Redmond, had been imprisoned on the *Captivity*, a prison ship in Portsmouth. He was released some time after March 18, 1810. Once again he was penniless and had no prospects. Mary Anne dreaded hearing from him again, but unknown to her, someone moved to help Redmond. She suspected it had been Buchan who prevailed upon Benjamin West to use James Barry's brother for the figure of the sick man in his heroic painting *Christ Healing the Sick in the Temple*. The money he earned gave Redmond the opportunity to make a fresh start. Soon after, he left England for the West Indies.

Mary Anne understood Daniel's concern about the steady flow of money, and she, too, worried about the amounts they were spending. "Daniel is right, you know," she told her daughter. "Once the money from my brother's pictures is gone, there isn't anythin' more. I thought we could count on the sales of the etchin's and the books, but no one seems to want them—and they've cost us money besides."

"Don't fret," Margaret replied. "As soon as I finish my degree, General Miranda will find a place for us in Venezuela. Doctors make lots of money, so we won't have to worry about it ever again."

"I'm sure you're right," Mary Anne said. "It's just that it's hard to find enough to pay off the bills, what with all the things you're needin' for school and all." Privately Mary Anne worried on another score as well. What if—heaven forbid it should happen—but what if the girl's disguise was discovered? She would immediately be thrown out of the university. Then there would be no job with General Miranda and no Venezuela. Meanwhile the money they were spending on educating Margaret could be put towards a dowry that might help her make a worthwhile marriage. Mary Anne supported her daughter with all her heart, but sometimes she questioned what the girl was doing. Wasn't marriage so much easier? It was what most women did. Why, then, wouldn't Margaret even consider it?

Mary Anne seemed not to realize that her own marriage and her son John's marriage each provided a frightening example for the young girl. Mary Anne had denied Jeremiah, just as John had denied his family. That wasn't what Margaret wanted in her future. And surely there was a reason none of her uncles had married. From Margaret's point of view, there was a definite shortage of happy marriages in her family. Much better to depend only upon herself. Then she wouldn't be vulnerable to the whims of others.

Margaret knew her mother wouldn't understand, even if she could explain it. So she just smiled and reassured the older woman. "You'll see," she said, patting her mother on the shoulder. "General Miranda has given us his promise, and he is a man of honour. All that really matters now is getting through my studies. Once I've earned my degree, our troubles will be over."

Mary Anne nodded and whispered a prayer that her daughter was right. It was good to think so, but still there was a little niggle in the corner of her heart, a small whisper of worry that things might not be as easy as her daughter thought.

"There's another thing, too," Margaret continued. "I won't have to wear men's clothing anymore or keep up this ridiculous pretense any longer. I can even let my hair grow back in. And best of all, I won't have to call you Mrs. Bulkley anymore."

Margaret's sally brought a smile to Mary Anne's face. "Well, I'll not deny 'twill be music to my ears to hear you say Mam again."

Late in the spring the university closed, and its students

returned to their homes. For Margaret and her mother, this was a difficult time. Crossly her mother insisted they return to London, where she could look after her business more forcefully.

"Daniel Reardon has still not sold those books or my parents' property in Cork. If I were there I could do something to help things along. Sittin' here a-writin' one letter after another isn't solvin' our problem."

But Margaret didn't want to go back to London. She preferred to stay in Edinburgh to continue her studies, either on her own or with a tutor. There was still so much she had to do. Her marks were good, but she felt others in the class were ahead of her. They had many years of schooling leading up to university. She did not. She still had much to catch up on.

Finally they appealed to the Earl of Buchan. "I'll abide by his decision," Margaret told her mother. Buchan suggested a compromise. He contacted a friend and scholar, Dr. Robert Anderson of Edinburgh, and arranged to have Margaret board at his home while Mary Anne returned to London. Buchan even helped defray expenses, sending two billets to Anderson, "recommending him [Barry] more particularly to your attention."

Later he called on Anderson again, asking another favour on Margaret's behalf. "It will be kind in you and Dr. Irving to look at the Latinity of his Thesis," Buchan wrote. "Tho' he is much younger than is usual to take his Degree in Medecine [sic] and Surgery yet from what I have observed likely to entitle himself to them by his attainments.

"He means to go by invitation of General Miranda to the Caracas."

At the end of the summer Mary Anne returned to Edinburgh and once again resumed her role as Mrs. Bulkley, the housekeeper. Soon after, Margaret received a letter from General Miranda confirming their plan. He planned to set sail for Venezuela late in October. He repeated his instructions to her: she was to follow him to Caracas as soon as she had obtained her medical degree.

Early in 1811 Margaret brought home more exciting news. "Look!" she cried. "Just look at the newspaper. General Miranda is in Venezuela!"

True to his promise Miranda had arrived in his homeland and begun the campaign to free his country from its oppressors. He had arrived in Caracas in December 1810 on board the British ship *Avon*. The welcoming committee that greeted him included Simon Bolivar, an old friend, said to be a fellow member of the Logia Lautaro. Over the years, they had corresponded back and forth, laying plans and sharing dreams. Now it was time for action.

There was much for Miranda to take in. It had been forty years since he had seen his homeland, and many things had changed in that time. But one thing remained the same: Venezuela was still under the heavy thumb of Spain.

Miranda quickly took up his revolutionary cause. He published articles and essays, circulated through the coffee houses and social groups, and used every opportunity he could to rally people to his cause. He found many like-minded people who supported him in his quest for political freedom. He consolidated this support into a Patriotic Society and was quickly elected president.

Margaret followed his progress through newspaper reports. That summer there was more good news to share with her mother. "Listen to this story in the newspaper. On July 5, Venezuela declared her independence from Spain. He's done it, Mam! Miranda is in command of the country. Oh, it will be so wonderful there. I can hardly wait!"

She looked at her mother. With all Margaret's work and all her studies, she had not noticed the steady change in her mother, who had grown weaker by the day. Margaret realized her mam looked suddenly older—old beyond her years and frailer than she had realized.

"You'll see, Mam. Soon we can leave Scotland and join him in Venezuela. It's going to be warm there, not like this damp and drafty country. The sunshine will warm your bones and you won't be cold any longer. You're going to love Venezuela."

Like her mother, Margaret missed the gentle climate of Cork. The sheltered waters of the southern coast kept it warmer than most of Ireland. The estates of some of the fine lords and ladies had fancy gardens with palm and eucalyptus trees. Many other subtropical shrubs and flowers flourished in these gardens. But palm trees could never grow in Edinburgh, she knew.

In fact Margaret knew little about Edinburgh. There had not been much time for her to explore the bustling city, to wander through the fields surrounding it or even to visit the great museums and galleries. Between studying, caring for patients and assisting the doctors at school, Margaret was busier than ever.

Each new term brought more equipment and supplies to buy, more bills to pay. Now even Margaret was alarmed at their rate of spending. Money was flowing away like a river in spring flood. Just when they needed more than ever, it became harder and harder to get any money at all from Daniel Reardon.

"I wish he'd sell those books," Mary Anne complained. "Write again and ask if he's sold my parents' house yet!"

This time Margaret shook her head. "If he sells anything he'll send us the money. He knows we need every penny we can get. There's no use harassing the poor man. We've a few things we could sell to tide us over. Now that spring is here we won't need our heavy winter clothing anymore, and next year we'll be in Venezuela. We won't need heavy cloaks and jackets there! If we take them down to the pawnshop, we might be able to get a few pounds for them. And I can sell some of my books to the junior students."

She was struck with another idea. "I just had a thought: I'm sure I could make some extra money tutoring as well. Some of those dunderheads sleep through class and then wonder why they don't do well on exams. They're always asking me for tutoring, but I've turned them down so far. With the final exams in sight, I'm sure there won't be any problem finding a few classmates who can pay good money for extra lessons. Don't worry. We'll get through it somehow."

We're almost there, she told herself. Only a few more months to go.

Then on Holy Thursday, March 26, 1812, as Margaret approached the final weeks of her studies, a devastating earthquake rocked Venezuela. Damage totalled more than four million dollars—billions in today's currency. More tragically the Venezuelan troops who were to defend their country against a threatened invasion by Spain were trapped inside their barracks during the earthquake. Heavy stone walls collapsed inward. Almost all of the soldiers were killed in the space of a few terrifying minutes. Spain took advantage of the chaos and tragedy to launch its threatened invasion. The handful of troops left in Venezuela couldn't defend themselves against the powerful Spanish army.

Worse, rumours soon spread that the earthquake was the act of God's own hand, punishing Venezuela for rising up against the might of Spain. Demoralized Venezuelans turned against the freedom fighters, adding their anger to Spain's mighty blows.

Puerto Cabello, the strategic centre of the Venezuelan uprising, surrendered. Miranda knew this was the decisive stroke in the battle. "I cannot cause further bloodshed in a hopeless situation," he told his aides. "I will withdraw the rest of my forces and release the men from their pledges. They are free to return home and make what they can of their lives."

Miranda wanted to spend one last night in his homeland—a night of prayer, of remembrance, and a chance to say farewell to his dreams. But he waited one night too long. He was betrayed. Someone led Spanish soldiers to the lonely spot where Miranda sat. Quickly they captured and arrested him.

The revolution was over.

Chapter Five

GRADUATION

MARGARET'S FIRST THOUGHTS were for General Miranda. After all the wonderful things he had done, all the plans he had made, after all his hopes for the people of Venezuela—after all that, why did his dreams have to end this way?

Her mother, more practical than Margaret, looked beyond Miranda's tragedy. "Sure, and it's a sad day for the general, true enough. But have you given thought to your own future? What will you be after doin' now that the general can no longer help you? Where will you go?"

Margaret stared at her mother in shock. At that moment she realized the safe haven of which she had dreamed was now completely and totally gone. All her carefully laid plans had been destroyed along with Miranda's.

Suddenly the long struggle to enter the university, the continuing scrabble for money, the hours of study required to keep up with other, better educated students, readying herself to meet the physical and mental demands of her profession— all seemed useless. There would be no place to use her hard-won skills. She no longer had a future.

Now it was Mary Anne who refused to give up.

"We've gone along this far," she told her daughter. "We're that near to the endin'. There's nothing else you *can* do but finish your studies."

"But to what end?" the girl cried. "Who will hire me once

they find out I'm a woman? No one. My future is as dead as the general's revolution."

"*Sin amhrán deas.** Is this my brave girl I'm hearin'? Maybe now's the time to forget about the lessons you've been learnin' at the university and think on the general's lessons instead. What would he be tellin' you if he were here? I'm thinkin' he wouldn't want you to quit."

Margaret's head reeled. Her mind was blank. What *would* he do? She couldn't begin to imagine. Wordlessly she shook her head. "I don't know," she whispered. "I just don't know."

Mary Anne looked at her daughter thoughtfully before she spoke. She remembered the swirling void that blanked out her mind when her son's actions sent her husband to jail and her to the streets. She remembered weighing factors, grasping at straws, trying to salvage her marriage and her life. She remembered the first time her lips formed the word *widow* when she repudiated her husband. Mary Anne could be tough-minded when necessary. Now she wondered if her daughter had that same quality.

"You can't be General Miranda's surgeon, that's true," she said slowly. "But who's to say you can't become a surgeon with some other army instead? Sure, and I'm thinkin' the British army needs doctors just as much as any other army."

Margaret's jaw dropped. Here? In England? She would be found out and become a laughing stock like those poor deluded women who joined the army to follow their lovers. No! That would never work.

Angrily she turned away and picked up one of her books, snapping the pages open. But her eyes refused to focus. Print danced over the page, spinning around in tight circles, just as her mother's words spun round and round in her mind. Was the idea so impossible? Could it work? Every army needed

**That's a nice song.*

doctors. That much she knew. Other women had joined the army or navy, but their disguises never lasted for long. They were usually found out when they were wounded in battle or gave birth to a child. Often it was the doctor who first learned their secret.

Soldiers and marines were examined and treated by doctors, but who examined the doctors? No one. And doctors were seldom on the field of battle, so they were rarely wounded. Maybe it wasn't such a crazy idea after all.

It would be too difficult if she stayed in England. She would be too close to too many people. But it might be possible in the colonies. There were fewer people there for one thing. And troops moved around from one post to another. It would not be like living in one place in England, where you came to know your neighbours and made close friends. Friendships were too dangerous for someone trying to conceal such a secret. And romance would be impossible. There could be no hope of marriage for her, but she had no plans in that direction in any case.

The more she thought about it, the more possible it became. If she joined the colonial forces and lived as a bachelor, she might just be able to avoid discovery.

There were other factors that could tip the scales in her favour as well. She knew that a surgeon held the rank of officer. Officers had better accommodations—and larger allowances. She could keep her mother with her as a housekeeper, just as she did now.

Still, she couldn't ignore the dangers, and there were many. It would mean continuing her disguise—not for a few months or a few years but for a lifetime. It would be a gamble with high stakes. If she were discovered she would lose everything. But she would have nothing at all if she didn't at least try. Was it worth the risk?

Each time she found one thing in favour of the plan, she

found another against it. But always there was the fact that she loved medicine and particularly surgery. It was something she felt born to do. Where, as a woman, could she find anything to compare with the wonderful sense of healing and power that medicine provided?

"You've done it this far," her mother said. "You're not only disguised as a man, you've turned yourself into a Londoner as well. If you can do that much, the rest should be easy."

Margaret turned again to face her mother. Brightening, she gave her a quick hug. "Mrs. B., I think it might just work." Margaret caught the quick grimace that crossed her mother's face and she laughed. "I know. You hate being called Mrs. B., but there won't be any choice. You realize that, don't you? That I can't call you Mam?"

Reluctantly her mother nodded. "Aye. But I must admit it's been music to my ears the few times you've slipped and done so. But no matter. Mrs. B. will do."

"I know," Margaret said. "I was looking forward to leaving old Mrs. B. behind, too. But if we can't, well, we'll just have to accept it." She paused for a minute, trying to gather her thoughts. "The more I think about it, the more I realize you're right. We don't really have a choice, do we? Will you help me for just a little while longer? It isn't as if I have that much to lose anyway. All they can do is drum me out. They can't hang me!"

"There's another thing to think about," Mary Anne added. "The general might be able to escape. He won't have his soldiers with him, but a man like that doesn't give up easily!"

Margaret brightened. "That's true, isn't it? He's escaped before and started all over again. You're right, Mam. I'm giving up too easily. You asked me to think of what he would do if he were in my shoes. Now I must think about what I would do if I were in his shoes."

Suddenly the girl laughed. "There's no doubt at all. If I were the general I'd do everything in my power to escape. And once I was free I'd start building my army again." Gleefully she clapped her hands together. "Once I had my army I would pursue the cause of freedom!"

"Sure, and you'd need your trusty doctor by your side," Mary Anne added, caught up in her daughter's enthusiasm.

Once again Margaret plunged into work on her thesis, the lengthy in-depth discussion of a medical problem that consumed the waking hours of graduating students. Every candidate for a medical degree had to write a thesis. It had to be an original work, focus on a medical problem, be completely accurate and carefully researched. More, it had to be written entirely in Latin. After the written work was finished, examiners would read and question her about it. These were the "orals" that everyone dreaded. The orals also were conducted completely in Latin. Questions were asked and responses were expected in that language. Not only that, but the Latin responses had to be free from grammatical errors and correctly pronounced.

"I'll never do it," Margaret groaned after another all-night session on the problem. "It's too hard."

Once again the Earl of Buchan came to her rescue. At intervals he invited Margaret to dinner at his Edinburgh estate, Dryburgh. During one of these evenings she expressed concerns about writing an entire thesis in Latin and then defending it in that language.

"Not to worry," he told her. "Keep working at it, do your best and I or one of my friends will read it before you submit it. We can quiz you on it as well, just for practice." Margaret was relieved. The earl was something of a Latin scholar and had published a Latin circular in *Gentleman's Magazine,* to which he was a frequent contributor.

Conversation around the table moved to other subjects.

Buchan was involved in another project, one of the many grandiose schemes that occupied his attention. To show his admiration for Sir William Wallace, Buchan had decided to place a huge statue of the Scottish leader on the top of a hill on the grounds of Dryburgh. He had already commissioned the statue and made arrangements for construction of a pedestal. He planned to put the statue in place on September 22, 1814, with suitable ceremony. "That will be the anniversary of Wallace's victory at Stirling Bridge," he explained.

Margaret held back a smile. It seemed the Scots had long memories. Wallace's victory had taken place on September 22, 1297—more than five hundred years earlier!

Once again money problems distracted Margaret from her studies. This time her mother, unhappy with responses to her letters, decided to return to London and speak with Daniel. If necessary she meant to stay there until the problem was resolved. She left in May 1812, and Margaret stayed behind to complete the final draft of her thesis.

The most difficult part had been choosing a topic. At first, like most of her classmates, she was at a loss for a subject. Theses had to be of genuine importance, and selecting a worthwhile topic was essential. The answer, when it occurred to her, was both bold and ingenious. What better way to make sure no one suspected she was a woman than by choosing the most masculine topic she could find! A common complaint among male patients was hernia of the groin. It was a distinctly masculine problem and would make the perfect topic for her thesis. It was certainly something no lady would ever discuss!

Margaret assembled her notes, which covered research up to the present, and began forming a premise based on her own observations. Now she had to gather that information together and meld it into a coherent whole. She wrote page after page of notes and outlines, writing and rewriting paragraphs and polishing her text.

"Someone could do a good thesis on writer's cramp," she complained, once again massaging her aching hand and shaking life back into her fingers. The narrow goose-feather quill sent pins and needles through her hand after an extended session of writing.

At last she was happy with her notes. Smiling, she dipped a freshly sharpened quill into the inkpot and carefully wrote the title: *Disputatio medica inauguralis, de merocele, vel hernia crurali.** Thoughtfully she penned another inscription, dedicating the work to General Francisco de Miranda and to David Stuart Erskine, the Earl of Buchan. Then came a quotation from Menander: "Do not consider my youth, but consider whether I show a man's wisdom."

She smiled as she began the next-to-last copy of the complete text. This one would go to Dr. Robert Anderson, her mentor and friend. He and Dr. Irving would examine it for errors in Latin as Buchan had requested.

With their comments before her, she began the final copy of her text, carefully slowing her hand to ensure that her words were clear and legible. Margaret's frayed temper erupted frequently during the weeks she spent copying, especially when her quill blasted a splatter of ink, spoiling the appearance of a page. The thesis was forty pages long. At times it seemed she would never finish. Each day she found minor changes she could make and better ways to present her ideas.

"If I'd just copy it and stop changing things, I'd be done in no time," she muttered, as she began rewriting yet another section. Still, she would write only one thesis, and this was the culmination of her university studies. The perfectionist in Margaret goaded her, and she doggedly plodded through page after page of copying. Others might hire penmen to do their copy work, but she alone would be responsible for hers,

An initial discussion of the femoral hernia or hernia of the groin.

and she would be familiar with every word in it when she met the challenge of her oral examination.

While Margaret worked on her thesis, her mother continued to search for markets for paintings, etchings and books, and for ways to somehow dispose of the Barry property in Cork.

The money they hoped for from James Barry's estate was slow to materialize. *Birth of Pandora*, one of the large paintings, had been put up to auction and sold for 230 guineas. It was a small fortune to Margaret and her mother. But the purchaser changed his mind, did not claim the picture and it was returned to Mary Ann.

Once again Margaret wrote to her cousin. "Please send £80 as soon as possible. I have the most urgent necessity for the money. Do not delay as it is of the greatest moment and any disappointment now would crush to the ground all our prospects. Next July will, please God, put an end to all my extraordinary expenses in Edinburgh."

At last the long awaited day arrived. Margaret's thesis was accepted. She completed and passed her final examinations and her orals. She was ready to receive her degree.

As she dressed for the ceremony, she was in a dreamlike state. It was hard to believe she had actually come to the end of her studies. She had reached her goal. Her thoughts turned again to General Miranda. "I wish he could be here," she whispered to herself. "Without him, this would never have been possible." She thought of her other sponsor, the Earl of Buchan, and mulled over the letter she would send to him. He had made it possible for her to enter the university and had been unstinting in his support over the years. She was deeply grateful and wanted to let him know just how vital his assistance had been.

Slowly she put the billowing black gown over her regular clothing. Her only disappointment was that Mary Anne would not attend the ceremony. They had discussed it earlier. Parents and guardians were welcome, but it would be strange to invite a housekeeper. There was another reason as well. Mary Anne's palsy by this time was well advanced. It was not easy for her to get around anymore. The physical effort of walking to the university and standing through the ceremony would be almost impossible for her.

"Darlin', I'm that proud of you my heart is about to burst. It's probably just as well I won't be there. I don't think I could hold back me tears, and wouldn't that be a sight—an old housekeeper bawlin' her eyes out over a young gentleman graduatin'? No, 'tis better if I stay here. Off with you now. Your friends will be waitin'. Just remember to tell me all about it when you come home."

As she walked to the university for the last time, Margaret waved to a few students. Most were surrounded by a cluster of people, but there was no group of celebrants for her. Aside from her mother, none of her family was aware of what was about to happen. The circumstances of her life were such that she had no close friends. It was a poignant moment. During the ceremony, as each graduand approached the podium and knelt to receive his doctoral hood, a burst of pride warmed Margaret's heart as she thought about her accomplishment.

What would they think, she wondered, if at this moment I proclaimed myself a woman? What a stir that would make! For half a second she was tempted but quickly smothered the impulse. There would be ample time to proclaim her true sex when she succeeded professionally and made a name for herself—or when General Miranda regained his freedom and resumed his cause.

Soon after graduation Margaret and her mother prepared to return to London. One by one they examined their small treasures and handful of possessions, deciding which could be sold and which should be packed away in chests for transport to London. Carefully Margaret sorted through her books. It was the one point on which she and her mother argued.

"Surely you'll not be needin' all those heavy books anymore," Mary Anne complained. "You've read them all and know them inside out. Why drag them around with us?"

But Margaret valued books too highly to part with them easily. A few she did give up, putting them aside to sell. The remainder she kept as reference texts. The precious survivors were packed in sturdy boxes. All too soon their few remaining belongings were sold or given away. Finally they watched a coachman strap their small collection of trunks and boxes on the back of a carriage, then climbed aboard and began the trip back to London.

The city was busier than either Margaret or her mother remembered and seemed to have grown in the few years they had been away. Once again there were lodgings to be found, but this time Margaret made the enquiries. Looking and sounding like a young Englishman, she had no trouble finding a place for herself and her Irish housekeeper.

"You know, Mam, I'm not quite ready yet to begin my practice," she told her mother soon after their arrival. "If I'm to succeed as I wish, I'll need more studies."

Mary Anne was aghast.

"After all that studyin' you're wantin' more? What more is there to learn?"

Margaret explained carefully why further study was truly important. If she was to be a really fine surgeon, one who was above all suspicion, she would need more study. There was no point in doing it any other way. General Miranda and the Earl of Buchan had both told her time and time again that it wouldn't be enough just to qualify, that she had to have top honours and a reputation that would not only withstand challenges but guard her against them.

Right now she rated herself as just average—better than

some, but nothing special. In her heart she knew she was not yet ready for unsupervised practice on living patients. There were still too many things she did not know, too many procedures she had not fully mastered. What she needed to improve her skills was postgraduate work in surgery. And, she decided, it couldn't be with just any surgeon.

"If he'll accept me, I've decided to apply to Sir Astley Cooper," she told her mother.

"And who's he?" Mary Anne demanded.

"He's the best surgeon in all of England," Margaret replied.

Somehow Mary Anne managed to coax some extra money from her cousin, and Margaret enrolled in Astley Cooper's classes. Once again she threw herself into her studies and read furiously, far into the night.

"Margaret, you'll be ruinin' your eyes with all that readin' by lamplight. Put it away and come to bed," Mary Anne insisted as night after night the girl pored over her books.

"In a bit, Mam," she replied. "I just want to go over this once more to make sure I've got it fixed in my mind."

Once again she rose to the top of the class and became a pupil dresser, a position that brought several privileges. Pupil dressers ranked somewhere above ordinary students and below the surgeon's apprentices. They either assisted the surgeons at the operating table or sat in reserved seats in the front row of the operating room, where they could watch the surgeon closely.

Margaret knew it was important to be as near to the operating table as possible. Surgeons operated very quickly and unless you were up close, you could not always see what they were doing. General anaesthetics were not yet available, and surgery was a painful procedure. Many would-be surgeons lacked the nerve to operate on fully conscious patients, but Margaret learned to be as quick and gentle as she could. She smiled to herself as she repeated a compliment one of the surgeon instructors had given her. "You have the hand of a woman," he said. "You should do well as a surgeon."

The insignia of surgeons included a woman's hand, signifying a gentle touch as well as dexterity and flexibility. That was a fine bit of irony. Her hands were welcome, but the rest of her wasn't. Had the instructor known Margaret really *did* have the hands of a woman, she would have been dismissed immediately.

For all her bravado, Margaret, along with most beginning surgeons, found it difficult to steel herself against patients' reactions: the fear and panic betrayed in their eyes, the involuntary flinching of muscles and the groans that escaped their lips. No matter how brave they tried to be or how hard they tried to hide their fear, it was a living presence in the operating room.

"Without the operation they can't be helped," she told her mother. "I know it's painful for them for a few minutes, but the results are worth it. It's as hard for me to inflict pain as it is for them to bear it, but I know in the long run I am helping them. As long as I remember that, I can close my eyes to their cries and concentrate on operating quickly and cleanly." Still, in difficult cases, Margaret, like her colleagues, was happy when the patient fainted. It made things easier for both.

Margaret and her mother lived near Southwark High Street, where the united teaching hospitals of Guy's and St. Thomas's were located. Surgical students such as Margaret could enter both hospitals, but medical students were allowed only in Guy's.

Like all students Margaret had to spend some time in residence at the hospital. Each residency lasted for an entire week. As the duty dresser she had a private sitting room and bedroom at the hospital for her exclusive use. The private sitting room was a prized perk. It meant she could relax and work at her studies and case reports without being bothered. And the privacy lessened chances that her secret might accidentally be uncovered.

At Guy's and St. Thomas's, Margaret behaved more like a doctor than she had done in Edinburgh. Here residents could treat some patients on their own. It was up to them to decide if they needed to call in a senior surgeon or not. The residents quickly developed reputations for their work. Some, with more bravado than others, refused to call in a senior surgeon at any time. Sometimes they were successful, but at other times the patient paid for their pride. A few of the residents tended to call for help at the first sign of a problem. Their patients were protected, but the residents did not learn how to cope with emergencies on their own. The majority of students fell somewhere between these two extremes.

Sometimes Margaret worked until two or three o'clock in the morning or even later because residents were required to remain on duty until all patients had been cared for. But it was wonderful training.

"I wouldn't have missed it for anything," she told her mother. "Studying from a book or listening to a lecturer is one thing, but here I am truly learning how to be a doctor."

Margaret's world was exciting, and she loved the challenges she faced. Daily she felt her skills improving. Both her surgical techniques and her diagnostic abilities surged ahead during her time with Astley Cooper.

Mary Anne was bewildered by her daughter. Margaret had never worked so hard in her life nor kept such dreadful hours. Sometimes she scarcely had time enough to eat. But the girl almost glowed with happiness. Eventually the year came to an end. She had finished her surgical studies. But still she wasn't satisfied.

"What now?" Mary Anne asked. "Surely there's nothin' more left for you to learn?"

"There's always more to learn," Margaret replied. "Andrew Fyfe has accepted me as a private student in practical anatomy. He's the best anatomist in the world, and I'm very lucky."

Once again Margaret's behaviour set her apart from other students. Some didn't bother doing the dissections that Fyfe included as part of the course work.

"Ungh," one groaned, delicately holding his nose as he watched Margaret at the dissecting bench. "How can you bear to do something so messy and disgusting? It's quite unpleasant."

But to Margaret it was not messy, disgusting or unpleasant. It was fascinating to trace the slender filaments of nerve and muscle, and marvel at the complex interconnections in the body. Memorizing textbooks could never provide the depth of understanding that dissection gave. Nor could books prepare her for actual surgery. Margaret bit back a retort, calmly continued her dissections, then discussed her findings with Fyfe.

She read widely in the medical journals, paying attention to new ideas and theories, thinking about what they might mean in her practice and how they might be used in treating her patients. Slowly she began to form her own theories.

At last Margaret's studies with Fyfe ended. She faced her final hurdle. It was time to put her knowledge to work and find employment as a doctor and a surgeon. She applied to the Home Office for the position of medical officer with the British army.

The written examination was no challenge to Margaret, and she breezed through it easily. Along with all the required courses, Margaret had taken many optional courses. These included such things as midwifery and Fyfe's dissection course. The extra courses helped her score well on the army tests. Few candidates were as well prepared as she.

Now only one obstacle stood between her and the coveted army appointment. She had to undergo a physical examination given by an army doctor. Her heart thumped wildly when she presented herself at the appointed time. A clerk was there to check her name off a list and direct her towards a small office, where she could wait for the doctor. She sat straight in her chair, trying to look as tall as possible. To calm her nerves, she gripped the arm of her chair, but she grasped it so tightly her knuckles turned white. She cleared her throat, praying that her shaking voice would not show how nervous she was. The sound of footsteps nearing the door announced the approach of the doctor. Her ordeal was about to begin.

The examiner strode into the room, seated himself and took a moment to open the file on his desk and look at Margaret's records.

This is the moment for a diversion, thought Margaret, so she seized it by launching into a discussion of Sir Astley Cooper's latest surgical techniques. By keeping her examiner involved in conversation, she could use up most of her appointed time. Doctors always enjoyed talking about their specialities, and with a few careful questions she could encourage him to dwell on his own experiences in the field. When at the last he realized he had not yet given her a physical examination, she brazened it out.

"What, do I look ill to you? Here. I shall stick out my tongue if you wish."

The youthful candidate seated before the doctor was obviously in the peak of good health. More importantly this person was applying for service overseas and in the colonies. It was not always easy to recruit well-trained surgical doctors for duty outside of England. Nor was the applicant trying to purchase a commission. Merit alone would decide the outcome. The examiner could easily see that the candidate's credentials were considerably better than his own. A physical examination was obviously a waste of time.

He smiled and took the young surgeon's pulse before quickly deciding there were no physical problems. It took only a moment to check off the examination chart to match his observations, then to send the lad on his way. There were, after all, other people waiting to see him.

On July 5, 1813, Margaret Anne Bulkley entered army service as Dr. James Barry, temporarily assigned to Plymouth. Her life as Margaret Bulkley had ended.

Her next stop was the tailor, where she ordered her uniform. Soon after she dressed herself in new clothing—the uniform of an army officer. She showed it off to her mother.

"Look Mam," she smiled, twirling in a circle. "What do you think?"

Mary Anne smiled weakly. "Sure, and 'tis a handsome young gentleman you've become," she said. "I'm only sorry I'll not be with you on your big adventure. 'Tis an excitin' time you'll be havin', I'm sure."

Margaret dropped to her knees, grasping her mother's hand tightly in her own. "Don't say that, Mam," she cried. "You're going to get well again. Wherever I go you'll always come with me."

The older woman shook her head and gently reached out one palsy-stricken hand. Softly she placed it on her daughter's head. "No, my sweetin'. Not this time. 'Tis I who'll go and you who'll stay. And it breaks my heart. You're so young—so young and so alone. But you can do it, my Margaret. I'll not see it, but somehow I know you'll make it all worthwhile."

Mary Anne Bulkley's death sometime later was not unexpected. She had been in failing health for many years, but it was still a sad and difficult time for Margaret. "All that training and I couldn't even help my own mam when she needed me," she cried.

GRADUATION

Her memories of this time would always be bittersweet. She had achieved her goal. But the person who had helped and encouraged her the most was gone. Her mother would never enjoy the benefits of what they had accomplished, never see her daughter succeed in her chosen field and never share the excitement of travel to far-off places.

It was a lonely victory.

Chapter Six

CAPE TOWN

JAMES BARRY'S FIRST ASSIGNMENT was at the military hospital in Plymouth. She arrived full of hope and enthusiasm, looking forward to working with *real* patients and sharing the experiences of other doctors on staff. True, she would be the most junior member of the surgical team, but she was confident she could meet the challenges that lay ahead. It was an exciting prospect.

Jauntily she climbed the steps of the hospital, entered the doors and looked around. This would be her world, and she very much liked the look of it. It was markedly different from the teaching hospitals to which she was accustomed. Here doctors walked the wards unattended by gaggles of students. There were no hurried consultations on made up problems as doctors-in-training prepared for quizzes by their instructors. Nor were there "professional" patients in the wards who, for a few pennies, whispered details of their ailments to the student doctors. This was a *real* hospital, and she was part of it.

After a moment she approached the administration desk and asked the soldier seated there for directions to the office of the senior medical officer. She missed—or chose to ignore—the startled glances that met her request.

Soon she stood before the officer in her most erect military posture and presented her documents. She could neither miss nor ignore the glare he gave her. The man was agitated and thumbed repeatedly through her papers as though looking for secret information contained in them. Barry's heart beat wildly. Was something wrong? Had she forgotten an important document? Surely he knew of her appointment? Finally he rose from his chair and glowered at her.

"According to these papers, I am led to believe you are a qualified surgeon," he began.

"Of course," she agreed proudly. "You have the transcripts of my degree and my postgraduate work along with references from my mentors and professors."

"You are just a child," said the officer, making no attempt to conceal his anger. "I don't know who has put you up to this, but I don't consider it a very good joke. I'm a busy man, and this waste of my time is in very poor taste. I do not have time for this sort of nonsense. Please tell that to your colleagues."

With that he sat down. She was dismissed.

Barry's temper began to rise. Working hard to contain the stinging words that rose to her lips, she pointed to each of her documents. "As this paper clearly shows, I have graduated from the University of Edinburgh. And as this letter testifies, I completed a course of postgraduate study with Sir Astley Cooper. That letter corroborates my course of dissection under Andrew Fyfe. I believe you also have received notice of my appointment to the staff at Plymouth." She drew herself up to her full five feet, looked him in the eye and snapped, "I believe my credentials are in order, sir."

The discussion went downhill from there. The officer had no option but to accept her on staff. But he quickly wrote a letter of complaint to his commanding officer. "Such a young person should not be allowed to be a doctor," he argued.

The medical department of the war office rejected his complaints. Barry had excellent qualifications, had done important postgraduate work and had been accepted by their office. The commanding officer was to put aside his prejudice and make a place on staff for Dr. Barry.

It was a poor start and Barry knew it. But she had no idea what she could do to improve the situation. The other doctors on staff—especially the older doctors with many years of experience—were of the same mind as their commanding officer. Barry looked like a child. It was impossible to have confidence in someone so young and so inexperienced. Furious, she swallowed their gibes and insults, and determined to show them she was not only as good as them but better.

Soon they had to admit her skills were commendable, but they did so grudgingly. Outside of the hospital environment they shunned her. Inevitably their attitude was reflected by the rest of the staff, even down to the male orderlies who nursed the patients. They took their own time in carrying out Barry's orders.

"I might have to put up with poor treatment by my peers and by my commanding officer," she muttered to herself, "but by heaven I do *not* have to put up with insubordination from orderlies." Soon the corridors rang with screaming confrontations as she insisted the orderlies follow her orders both exactly and promptly.

"Who does he think he is?" grumbled one orderly, stinging from a scathing rebuke.

"I don't know," muttered another, "but I'm not letting myself in for another session like that." Gradually the orderlies treated her with military correctness and followed her instructions to the letter.

Now she understood why Buchan and Miranda had insisted that she had to excel in her studies and why nothing less than first-class marks were acceptable. For the first time she wondered if they had somehow guessed that her qualifications and abilities would be so severely challenged and had foreseen how very difficult it would be for her to find acceptance.

They never warned her about this aspect of the challenge, she mused, although in all fairness, they had never planned for her to practise like this. "These hidebound traditionalists don't have to like me," she decided, "but they *will* have to respect me and let me do my job."

Margaret thought often of General Miranda. She still dreamed of Caracas. "None of this would have happened if Miranda's plans had worked out," she sighed and redoubled her efforts to be letter-perfect in her job. Venezuela was still a possibility if Miranda could make his escape. Ardently she hoped their dream might still come true. He had escaped once before when he was imprisoned in Cuba. It could happen again. In the meantime she was gaining experience that would make her more valuable to Miranda when he was finally free.

Barry continued to press for an overseas posting, and at last her request was granted. One of her dreams was about to come true. Like her brother, John, and her uncles, she was going to a far-off exotic place. Her orders sent her to the British colony of Cape Town in South Africa.

In preparation for her adventure she gathered her possessions around her and examined each carefully. There was not much to deal with. There was little left of her former identity as Margaret Bulkley. Only a few small keepsakes—such as the mourning brooch of her mother's hair—and these were placed in a small black metal box. She sorted once again through her books and looked carefully at her medical kit and instruments. It was hard to know what she might need until she arrived in Cape Town. One thing was certain: the climate in Cape Town would be warmer than that of Plymouth. She could discard the few remaining warm cloaks and jackets she had brought from Edinburgh. Everything else—her bits of furniture, her blankets, bedding, dishes and pots, all her household goods—she sold.

Barry preferred to make a clean break with her past, and as she prepared to leave Plymouth, she cut the last of her family ties. The printed books of her Uncle James' etchings and the originals went to Daniel Reardon to dispose of as he would. Whatever money they brought would be his, a small return for all the kindnesses he had shown Margaret and her mother. It was too dangerous to let Reardon know where she was going and, more importantly, *who* she was. For the sake of a few pounds from her uncle's books, she didn't want to take a chance on anyone discovering her true identity. She packed the last of her things into an old tea chest and addressed it to Daniel at Corbet Court in London.

She did not know how to contact her brother. She did not even know if John had finally married Kate Ward. But, really, it didn't matter. Her new life would not permit any contact with her family again.

The voyage to Cape Town was almost sixty-two hundred miles. She prepared herself for a boring trip lasting many weeks. Along with her medical books she packed some lighter reading material, which was always in short supply in the colonies. A new edition of Jonathan Swift's works, including *Gulliver's Travels*, had just been published. She looked forward to reading it along with a number of other books she hadn't had time for over the past months.

To her surprise, however, there was little time for reading. There was too much to see and too much to think about for boredom to be a problem. Barry had never travelled outside of Great Britain. Now she had the world before her. As the ship slipped past Morocco, Mauritania and along the coast of Africa, past the British colonies of Gambia and Guinea, she saw for the first time the lush tropical growth that offered a hint of what was to come. Days and nights grew warmer as the ship continued its southward progress. Gradually the long daylight hours grew shorter as they headed towards the equator, where the days were divided equally between light and dark. There was almost no twilight or dawn. It was completely unlike anything she was used to.

In the evening hours, passengers often stood by the ship's rail, savouring the soft warmth of the tropical night while watching the peculiar luminescence of the water outlining the passage of some strange sea creature or simply lighting up the waves. At times balls of St. Elmo's fire danced from the spars.

She loved the soothing sound of water rushing by the ship's sides and the snap of canvas in the wind. There was a rhythm to the clanging of the ship's bells and an order to the routines of the sailors as they went about their chores, scrubbing the decks with holystones (soft sandstone blocks), responding to changes in wind, tides and weather, and checking ropes and knots on the running gear. In their spare time the mariners demonstrated surprising skills, carving bits of ivory, weaving ropes into Gordian knots that seemed to have no beginning or end and creating miniature sailing ships from whatever materials they had on hand.

As the ship moved towards the equator it turned away from sight of land and headed to the British colony of St. Helena. Between the last glimpse of land off Sierra Leone and the first sight of the tiny island colony, the ship would cross the equator, the invisible line that divides the globe into the northern and southern hemispheres.

A brisk knock on her door awoke the doctor that morning. "All out, all out, and pay homage to King Neptune," one of the sailors called.

Barry dressed quickly, not sure what was happening. On deck she found one of the seamen wearing a flowing robe and long white whiskers made from a mop. On his head he wore a gleaming crown that looked suspiciously like a pot from the galley, as the ship's kitchen was known. He sat on a throne made from a wooden barrel. Beside him stood an assistant dressed equally strangely. He carried a mug of shaving cream and a large bucket of sea water.

"What's this all about?" Barry asked, nudging a fellow

officer standing next to her along the ship's rail.

"It's a special ceremony for seamen crossing the equator for the first time," he explained. "Old King Neptune demands his due for every new sailor entering his realm. These mariners are a superstitious lot. I think they really believe something terrible will happen if they don't do this, and they'll tell you about the terrible fate that befell some poor ship whose captain thought it was nonsense.

"What usually happens is the captain retreats to his cabin and turns the ship over to the crew for an hour or so. That way he doesn't have to acknowledge that any of this nonsense has taken place, and he doesn't have to write it up in the ship's log. Some of the owners don't look kindly on losing time. From what I've seen it usually winds up with a few good-natured pranks, tots of rum all round and no harm done."

Barry watched, fascinated, while seamen crossing the equator for the first time were identified by their fellows, daubed with shaving cream, shaved with dull razors, doused with sea water and set to doing silly stunts to the accompaniment of loud laughter from the rest of the crew. Then, as her friend predicted, all hands enjoyed a ration of rum and toasted the health of both King Neptune and King George. Soon after, the bosun piped an end to the ceremony and regular shipboard routine resumed.

Luckily for Barry she was a good sailor. Seasickness devastated many of the passengers during the first weeks of the voyage. Not only were they physically ill, but they were ashamed of their illness and embarrassed if they were found out. Barry allowed herself a small chuckle. There really wasn't any way to hide seasickness, or *mal de mer* as some passengers preferred to call it. Giving it a French name didn't make it any less miserable. Barry asked the ship's doctor about treatments for the malady.

"There isn't any real cure," he replied, "except for dry land, of course. That works every time."

"Can't you give them anything?" Barry asked.

He shook his head. "Some of the sailors insist that drinking a pint of sea water calms the stomach, but that's pretty drastic. Ginger tea helps a little, as does eating dry ship's crackers if it's just a touch of seasickness. But for a really bad case, nothing helps. I've seen men try to throw themselves overboard to end their agony."

As the ship approached St. Helena, Barry wondered if she might catch a glimpse of the island's most famous prisoner. There was a flurry of interest among the passengers as the ship pulled into harbour, and a number of them stood along the rail, some with telescopes and looking glasses, peering anxiously at the little settlement to catch a glimpse of Napoleon Bonaparte. They were disappointed, however. The governor had ordered Bonaparte to stay in his quarters, safely out of view, whenever a ship arrived in the harbour.

The ship's captain went ashore only long enough to visit the garrison commander, deliver mail and orders from the Colonial Office and pay his respects to the governor, Sir Hudson Lowe. While the captain was occupied, a small group of crew members was authorized to land and replenish the ship's water supply. All others had to remain on board.

"They've turned the whole island into a prison," one of Barry's shipmates commented. "Old Bony won't be a threat to anyone ever again."

"I'm not so sure about that," another replied. "He's escaped from custody before, and he seems to have a magic touch when it comes to rallying supporters."

"That's true," the first responded. "And his tactics are brilliant. The man is a master of strategy. It was only the weather that defeated him in Russia."

"He came very close to ruling all of Europe," his companion agreed, "and I don't think they'll feel truly safe until he's dead."

Soon they were headed back out to sea on the last leg of the journey. Once the little island slipped into the sea behind them, they saw only ocean in every direction. Finally a sailor in the crow's-nest sang out the traditional cry, "Land ho!" Barry joined the other passengers who crowded the rail as Cape Town's famous Table Mountain emerged from the sea mist along the horizon. It was a familiar sight to some but brand new to others. It impressed both groups. Barry had read descriptions of the harbour, but to see it first-hand was thrilling.

The mountain looming behind the colony drew every eye. It appeared to be perfectly flat on top as though some giant had lopped it off with a knife. The shoulders of the mountain were scoured into gullies, enhancing their resemblance to table legs. Around its base the lush growth vividly contrasted their last glimpse of the English coast. Even the colour of the vegetation was different. Here there were a thousand shades of green, radiant and bursting with life. Brilliant flashes of colour punctuated the scene: the surrealistic-appearing flowers along with the bright reds, yellows and greens of tropical birds dramatically contrasted the subdued colours of the vegetation, pigeons and sparrows that teemed in London's parks and gardens.

The ship's sails snapped like exploding fireworks as though the ship, too, were celebrating the end of the voyage.

It had been a long trip, thought Barry, as the vessel luffed and tacked through wind and waves on its journey from London to Cape Town. Barry had spent many of her daylight hours on deck, where she had gradually become accustomed to the view of endless waves flinging spume from their curling tops, ceaseless patrols of hungry gulls and albatross, and shimmering flights of flying fish. A soothing peaceful rhythm had become part of life aboard the ship, and after the intensity of the past year, Barry had been able to relax at last. The voyage had given her time to mourn for her mother, then move beyond her grief. She had put behind her the bitter experiences at Plymouth Military Hospital. As the voyage finally came to an end, a flush of excitement swept over her. Ahead lay a new adventure, a new beginning. She relished the thought of starting with a fresh slate.

Now her neighbour at the rail turned and spoke. "Remarkable, isn't it?" he said. "They say that during the rainy season the clouds drape themselves over the mountain like some giant tablecloth. It's easy to see how Table Mountain got its name! It's quite unlike any other skyline I've ever seen."

It would be exciting to climb that mountain, Barry thought, and wondered what she might be able to see from the other side. Certainly the mountains were nothing like the craggy hills in Scotland, such as Ben Niven, where people flocked on holidays to walk the well-defined trails. Nor was it anything like the rolling hills, clothed in soft green, that marked the countryside in her beloved Ireland. A whole new life awaited, and she tingled with anticipation.

As soon as the ship docked and the passengers disembarked, Barry found her way to the military hospital's headquarters and presented her documents. This time there were curious glances but none of the hostility she had encountered in Plymouth. She was assigned to her quarters, and while she waited for her trunks to arrive, she took the opportunity to wander around Cape Town, looking curiously at everything she saw.

Everywhere, the local people moved through the streets, carrying out their various tasks. Barry had seen very few Africans in London, and fewer still in Edinburgh or Cork. They were kept as slaves in some households, she knew, but rarely did they venture onto the streets. Now she gave her curiosity full rein and stared openly at the bustling crowds. She marvelled at the gleaming blackness of their skins in brilliant contrast to their colourful clothing. She looked at the baskets women carried, filled with exotic fruits and vegetables whose names she could not even guess. She listened to the melodious voices, speaking local languages as well as English, with accents that fell softly on her ears.

Everything was strange to her eyes. Gardens surrounding homes displayed a profusion of colourful flowers. A few she recognized but most were new and astonishing in their brilliance. Here and there a group of monkeys swung through the branches of trees or loped along the ground with their comical gait. It was almost a dream world, and her head reeled as she tried to take it all in.

She had time to wonder, as well, about the governor of Britain's colony at the southern tip of the African continent. In her pouch she carried a letter of introduction from the Earl of Buchan to Lord Charles Somerset. Both Buchan and Somerset claimed kinship with royalty. Neither were in line for the throne, but they were proud of their royal connections.

Buchan and Somerset had enjoyed a long friendship, and Barry looked forward to meeting the governor and his family. She had heard that Somerset's wife, the Lady Elizabeth, was ailing. It was an elastic term with many society women, some of whom thoroughly enjoyed ill health. It seemed to prevent them from doing things they didn't want to do but never hampered their search for pleasure. Nor did it affect their lifespans: some ailing women lived to a ripe old age. Soon enough she would meet the governor's wife and judge for herself to what degree Lady Elizabeth was actually incapacitated.

She knew of the governor's four children and laughed to herself when she first heard their names. Officially the governor represented the king, but seemed to want to represent the entire royal family by naming his children Georgiana for King George, Charlotte and Charles for King Charles, and Villiers

Plantagenet for the name carried by England's kings from Henry II to Richard II. In the latter case they were family names as well. Somerset was a direct descendent of the Plantagenet kings and a member of the Beaufort family, whose members had defended royal causes with their lives and fortunes.

Cromwell had ruined the Somerset family during his commonwealth era after the Civil War. Henry Somerset, the fifth Earl, had spent nearly two million pounds supporting the Stuarts and defended his castle at Raglan so stubbornly that it was the last estate to fall to Cromwell's men.

Restoration of Charles II to the throne returned the Somersets to a position of wealth and power. Barry knew the history of the Somerset family, but Buchan added some personal history as well. "Lord Charles' father was brought up at Badminton," he explained, referring to the vast country estate with a 116-room house set in parklike surroundings. Barry thought Somerset's father's romantic and impulsive youth was as interesting as a novel. He had rejected marriage to the heiress his parents chose for him. Instead he fell in love and eloped with Elizabeth Boscawen. The governor of Cape Town, Lord Charles Somerset, was the second son of that union.

"Lord Charles was just as impulsive and romantic as his father," Buchan told her. "He, too, fell in love—with a lady named Elizabeth Courtenay." She was one of the thirteen children of Viscount Courtenay of Powderham Castle. She was not penniless, but with so many brothers and sisters, her dowry and inheritance would be very small. History repeated itself. His parents urged him to look for someone with better prospects. Meanwhile the young couple told their parents they were attending a masquerade ball given by friends. They eloped to Gretna Green in Scotland, where they were married. The newlyweds eventually reconciled with their parents, and Somerset picked up the threads of the career that led to his appointment in South Africa.

Barry sighed at the romantic tale and looked forward to meeting Lord Charles and Lady Elizabeth. With Buchan's letter of introduction she also hoped to be invited to a few social events and make new friends in the colony.

About this time, Barry made a radical change in her diet. She became a complete vegetarian. She may have been inclined to vegetarianism earlier in her life, but the meals aboard ship had turned her away from eating meat. Well-cured meat, which could last for months, was so heavily pickled it was almost like eating leather. Poorly cured meat became a seething mass of maggots. Aboard ship cured meat was the only option, save giving up meat entirely. Besides, the profusion of fruits and vegetables in Cape Town was an irresistible temptation, especially following the limited shipboard menus of the past weeks.

Once Barry settled in her job, she was determined there would be no repeat of the Plymouth experience. She would show everyone just how good she was. Some of her patients wondered about her youth, but before long she won them over. Her treatments were effective. Her surgery was quick and clean. In Cape Town she encountered for the first time the tropical diseases she had read about, including yaws and jungle ulcers.

Despite her desire to gain the acceptance and respect of her peers, she could not hold her tongue when it came to the best treatments for her patients. She chaffed at the restrictions that, as a junior member of the surgical unit, limited her sphere. She fumed at the useless medications patients were fed. Most importantly she wanted to change conditions in the wards and give patients healthier diets. It was frustrating. She could suggest but not order. When her suggestions were ignored, she bided her time but made sure to implement as many changes as she could for the patients under her care.

"These doctors need to update their old-fashioned techniques," she grumbled to herself. "Some of them have never even heard the new theories about animacules* or about cleanliness in the surgical field."

On December 17, 1815, she earned her first promotion to staff assistant surgeon. She was still not completely comfortable with the older doctors. They weren't cruel, as the doctors at Plymouth had been, but some were slow to accept her and treated her as a youngster.

"I guess," she told herself, "to them I am a youngster. They expect me to respect them simply because they've been surgeons for thirty years. But they are so out of date I find it hard not to snatch the scalpel out of their hands and show them how it should be done."

About this time a ship arrived carrying a treasured packet of newspapers to the colony. But it was through these papers that Barry learned her dreams of Caracas were dashed. General Miranda had died on July 14, 1815. Now there was no hope at all that he might escape his prison and bring freedom to Venezuela—and to her. It was a final blow of irony that he had died on the twenty-third anniversary of the day the people of Paris stormed the Bastille during the French Revolution. Miranda had played a role in that struggle as well. Now his personal struggle was over, and she must carry on without his support and without the dream that had helped focus her energies during the difficult years in Edinburgh, London and Plymouth.

Choice had been taken from her. She had no option but to continue in the role that Buchan and Miranda had fashioned for her. But now she alone was responsible for her future.

Living her secret life was hard in small ways she had not anticipated. One of the most irksome was that she had no

*germs

confidante, no one with whom to share her innermost thoughts and dreams, no trusted friend who could be as close as a sister. In recent years her mother had been the only person she could entrust with her secrets. As her job grew more and more demanding, the loss of her mother's comforting presence was more sharply felt.

Now there was no one. It was hard not to have a close friend and always to be so careful of what she said. Some things she could discuss with her fellow surgeons, but there were other things that could never be mentioned. What she really needed was a silent companion, someone she could talk to but who could be relied upon never to repeat a word.

Still, other aspects of her life were very satisfying. She had finally met the governor, and she and Lord Charles became good friends. To the surprise of the military establishment, Somerset appointed her as his private doctor to care for him and his family. As the governor's doctor, Barry had a private house on the grounds of the governor's mansion and an annual salary in addition to her military wages. The privacy was as great a reward as the salary.

Once Barry was established, she began the first of a long series of campaigns to improve conditions for the troopers in the ranks and for the residents of the colony. Gradually her reputation grew and with it the demand for her services. Barry's income increased in swift leaps. In addition to consultant's fees, military salary and wages from the governor, she earned extra rixdollars (the currency of Cape Town) as surgeon and director of the Vaccine Institute, the colonial medical inspector, the superintendent of the leper institution and the medical officer of the town jail. She may have been one of the most highly paid women of her time.

After the penniless years in Cork, London and Edinburgh, Barry no longer had to worry about money. She had more than enough for her needs. "Ah Mam, I wish you were here now," she whispered. "It would do my heart good to buy a few luxuries for you."

Barry did buy a little pony for herself so she could ride comfortably around the colony. She needed help to mount a regular-sized horse, which was not only inconvenient but galled her independent spirit. The pony's smaller size meant she could mount and dismount by herself. She hired a black servant, John, to walk beside her pony holding a large parasol to shade her from the sun. The harsh rays of the African sun turned her pale skin lobster-red, and she suffered through several painful sunburns during her early days in the colony. She knew people laughed about her appearance, but if John and the parasol could protect her from future sunburns, she didn't care. John's duties were varied and included looking after her household and ensuring her comfort.

Sometime during this period she bought, or was given, the first of a series of little white dogs that would play an important role in her life. People laughed at the way she talked to her dog and carried it with her whenever she could. They didn't know it was her closest friend, the only living being she could depend on not to repeat her secrets.

"And no matter what other people say, no matter how they laugh at me, you still love me, don't you, Psyche?" she said, tousling the pup's hair and giving it a quick hug.

Each of her little dogs bore the same name—Psyche—and for the rest of her life, Psyche would always be close by. The name was a private joke. In medicine, psyche represents the soul, or the spirit. But in Greek mythology, Psyche is the beloved of Eros, one of the many Greek gods. She is usually depicted as a young girl with the wings of a butterfly. In choosing the name Psyche, Barry at once saluted her medical persona and, in the alter ego provided by the little white dog, recognized her femininity as well.

Cape Town was an interesting place. It was a mixture of

Dutch and English customs and languages. Barry was famil-
iar with the history of the Cape. It was founded by the Dutch
East India Company and later taken over by Great Britain.
British occupancy ended in February 1803, when the Peace of
Amiens awarded the colony to the newly created Republic of
Holland. Commissioner General Jacob Abraham de Mist and
General Jan Willem Janssens, appointed to head the new
government of the Cape, planned sweeping changes to rid the
colony of any lingering British influence.

Before these could take place, war broke out again. On
January 10, 1805, Britain once again took possession of the
African colony. The British had no intention of losing it a
second time.

When Somerset was appointed governor, he made a decisive move. Instead of retaining his true home and taking a
temporary residence so he could visit the Cape once in a
while, as many governors did, he established a genuine home
at the Cape for himself and his family. When his house was
completed he brought his family out from England. Slowly
the relationship between Barry, Somerset and his family grew
and deepened. No longer just their doctor, Barry became a
friend to each member of the family, and they returned that
friendship. In the warmth that surrounded her, Barry could
almost believe they were her real family.

But soon, just as in her previous life, the family was torn
apart. Barry had to talk frankly with Lord Charles. Lady
Elizabeth was not malingering or exaggerating her weakness.
She was not simply ailing, she was seriously ill. Sadly Barry
informed Somerset there was nothing more she could do for
his wife. All that was left was to make Lady Elizabeth as
comfortable as possible until the inevitable occurred. No
record remains of the exact cause of Lady Elizabeth's illness,
but Lord Charles was not surprised by Barry's words. Doctors
in England had held out no hope either. They, too, told him

it was simply a matter of time. But Lady Elizabeth wanted to come to Cape Town with him and see her children settled in their new home before she died. She was a courageous woman who did everything in her power to ensure that her family would be cared for after her death.

Even though it was expected, the governor was devastated by the loss of his wife. Some people expected him to move back to England, but he remained at the Cape. "I feel I am closer to her here," he told his friends. "This is my home now."

Barry, too, felt at home in the Cape settlement. She became a familiar sight to the local people, and her medical skills earned the gratitude of many families. Members of Cape society may have smiled at the figure the little doctor cut, but they were eager to invite her to their homes. Barry responded happily. She hired a local tailor to make new dress uniforms to wear for social engagements. They were regimental in design and colour, but the fabrics were unusual. She indulged herself in silk, satin and brocades with the sheerest of lawn stocks and shirts.

She was seen taking part in a busy round of dinners, dances and parties. She was a brilliant conversationalist and livened many a dinner table with stories of her adventures, some real and some imagined. Inevitably she found herself with invitations from the young ladies of the Cape to partner them at dances, card parties and other social events.

Before long she realized she was in trouble. Some of the young women—and their parents—began to look at her as a possible suitor. There was a shortage of socially acceptable young single men at the Cape, and even if Barry didn't have an illustrious family, she did have the sponsorship of men like Somerset and Buchan. She also had enough money to support a wife. Somehow she had to convince the young ladies and their parents that she didn't want to get married. But how?

"I can't afford to hurt their feelings," she confided to Psyche, "but I don't want to encourage them either."

Psyche had no answers to Barry's questions, and soon rumours began to circulate around the colony that the doctor was planning to marry first one, then another, of the lovely young heiresses. At one point an engagement was announced, but that relationship was quickly broken off.

Her social problems were perplexing, but they were minor matters compared to the medical challenges she faced. Her duties included caring for patients in the Cape's leper colony. Barry knew about Hansen's disease, or leprosy as it was called at that time. It was listed in the medical textbooks and had been an ancient scourge, mentioned in the Bible, that afflicted sufferers in tropical countries for uncounted centuries. There had even been a few outbreaks of leprosy in Europe although they were mostly confined to the warmer regions around the Mediterranean. Now she saw it for the first time.

Leprosy is a disfiguring disease that takes several forms. One strain begins with scaly patches on the skin that thicken and fold on themselves, eventually transforming the features of its victims and leaving them with a thickened nose and lionlike appearance. That aspect is accentuated by another quirk of the disease which thickens and coarsens the hair so it stands out around the head like a lion's mane. Another type of leprosy destroys feeling in the skin. Its victims are unable to feel damage to their fingers, hands, toes and feet, and often they ignore injuries, infections and other traumas, which can result in the loss of their appendages.

For Barry, one of the most horrifying aspects of this type of leprosy was that rats could eat victims' fingers and toes while they slept unaware of the rodents' attack. Equally troubling were the infections rats spread during their attack.

There were no known cures for leprosy. The only available

treatment was the application of an oil made by grinding the nuts of the chaulmoogra tree. Barry was not sure that chaulmoogra oil did anything at all to help those with leprosy, but there was nothing else to offer. At least it might help to soften their skin. It seemed to her that the leprosy must itch terribly, at least in the beginning stages. In the later stages, of course, the patients felt nothing at all.

By long-standing tradition, people with leprosy were placed in lifelong quarantine in isolated areas outside the city. They were forbidden to live with their families, to work in public places, to travel public roads. Barry was aware that lepers were considered outcasts, but when she made her first official visit to the Cape's leper colony, she could hardly believe her eyes. Her temper, always difficult to control, exploded in outrage at the conditions she found. "These poor people aren't responsible for their illness, yet they are treated like the worst of criminals," she told Somerset. Barry issued orders for the patients in the leper colony to be bathed daily, their sores bandaged properly and their diets improved to include fresh fruits and vegetables with lots of milk and clean water to drink.

Those responsible for the lepers were outraged and complained to Lord Charles, but it did them no good. He agreed completely with the doctor. Like Barry, he wanted to do everything he could to improve the living conditions of the lepers, whose affliction was no fault of their own. Barry's instructions were carried out. It improved the lot of not only the lepers, but also those few who chose to follow their loved ones into isolation. Several women placed their children with friends and family, then followed their husbands into the leper colony to help care for them. They knowingly placed themselves at risk but accepted that chance. Somerset's edict made life easier for them.

Lord Somerset's compassion stirred something in Barry's

heart. Barry discovered an increasing number of things they enjoyed in common. Both were emotional, and their actions were often dictated by their hearts, not their heads. Like Barry, Lord Somerset enjoyed books. And like Miranda, Somerset had an extensive library, which he invited Barry to enjoy. He did not limit his generosity to Barry but opened a public library, making books available to all members of the Cape Town colony. In later years he would expand his generosity, opening a museum to record and protect Cape Town's history. In dozens of ways Somerset demonstrated warm and winning qualities. He was a gentleman in the finest sense of the word.

Somerset was sorely grieved by the loss of his wife, and during this period he and Barry drew into a close friendship. The lively inquisitive young doctor seemed almost like one of his children, and Lord Charles frequently invited Barry to take part in family excursions. Her feelings for him deepened.

In 1817 Lord Charles set out on an expedition to explore first-hand the conditions on the Cape's troubled frontier. Somerset's two daughters were part of the group, along with Lieutenant Colonel Bird, the deputy colonial secretary; Captain Thomas Sheridan, the colonial treasurer and son of the famous playwright Richard Brinsley Sheridan; and Barry.

It was a wonderful adventure for Barry. The group stopped at Knysna, where they were hosted by the mysterious George Rex. "Have you heard what they say about George Rex?" Georgiana whispered to Barry. "They say he is the son of George III and the Quaker woman, Hannah Lightfoot."

It was commonly believed that Lightfoot and George III were married, but the royal house refused to recognize the young man's union with a commoner. If they had done so, their child, young Rex* would have been a prince and in line for the throne.

*"*king*" in Latin

Instead George Rex came to the colony in 1796 as marshal of the admiralty, serving until the Dutch occupation. At that time he retired to Knysna, maintaining a royal lifestyle on his twenty-five-thousand—acre estate.

During this trip Somerset also met with Gaika, one of the leading chiefs of the Xhosa. Lord Charles persuaded Gaika, Ndhlambie and several other chiefs to come to Grahamstown to trade, but in fact, Somerset was attempting to defuse a difficult situation. There had been frequent conflicts along the border between natives and settlers, often involving the theft of cattle. Lord Charles used every means he could think of to encourage peaceful relations, but at the same time, he established a series of fortified posts, staffed by more than one thousand soldiers, to patrol the area. He also formally agreed with Gaika to establish a neutral territory on the far side of the Fish River. This would provide an important buffer between the two factions.

Another problem loomed on the horizon as well. Shaka, leader of the Zulu nation, was becoming an increasing threat to peace in the region. Shaka had studied the actions of the British and Dutch troops and applied what he had learned, going far beyond the rigid confines of traditional European tactics. He was a brilliant strategist who deployed his men as curving horns, outflanking and surrounding his enemies. His actions demonstrated a keen understanding of guerrilla tactics as well. Shaka was the subject of several of Lord Somerset's exhaustive reports.

Throughout the trip, they marvelled at Somerset's ability to turn potentially explosive political conflicts into peaceful accords. Shaka may have been a brilliant strategist, but Somerset was a master of diplomacy. Upon their return to Cape Town, Barry knew just how lucky the Cape was to have Somerset, and her dedication to him became unswerving.

The following year Lord Charles' eldest son, Henry, was

posted to the Cape colony. He arrived on June 20, 1818, aboard the brig *Alacrity*. With him were his wife, Frances, and their only child. It was an emotional day for Lord Charles as he greeted his son and held his only grandson.

A few months later Lord Charles fell ill. Barry's diagnosis was typhus with complications. Somerset's condition was serious, and it took all of Barry's medical skills to bring him safely through his illness.

Once recovered, Somerset pursued his longheld dream of increasing the Cape's population. He was very specific in his choice of immigrants. The new land needed skills, not the unproductive presence of remittance men and younger sons. In 1819 parliament agreed to provide assisted immigration to the Cape. It was a wonderful opportunity to escape the depression that gripped Britain at the time, and over eighty thousand applied. They ranged from merchants and crafts-men to farm workers and army officers on half pay. The first two groups, each consisting of one hundred families, were to arrive early in 1820.

Late in 1819, not long before the first settlers were to arrive at the Cape, Somerset's eldest daughter fell ill. He requested an extended official leave to take her to England, and his request was granted. Major–General Sir Rufane Donkin was appointed acting governor in Somerset's absence. Donkin had recently left India after the death of his wife. He was a high-ranking officer with a good deal of administrative experience, and Somerset welcomed his appointment. He felt the colony would be in good hands during his absence.

On the surface, all seemed well. In London, Somerset worked for two years on the colony's behalf, purchasing breeding stock—cattle, sheep and pigs—to ship back to the Cape. He raised money for a church at Grahamstown and bought two of the newly invented threshing machines that were revolutionizing British harvests. He recruited teachers for the government schools and tended to other colony business as well.

His daughter's treatments went well, and with her recovery Lord Charles felt free to enjoy the London social season. Early in 1820 he met Lady Mary Poulett and began courting her. The following year they attended the coronation of King George IV on July 19, 1821. In August they were married at St. George's Church in Hanover Square, and in September at Plymouth they boarded the Royal Navy frigate *Hyperion,* bound for the Cape.

But things had not gone smoothly in the colony during Somerset's absence. Donkin had not followed the governor's plans. Among other things he had settled men and officers from the disbanded Royal African Corps in the neutral territory along the Fish River, violating Somerset's agreement with Gaika. He also had instituted a series of laws prohibiting settlers from leaving their settlements without written passes and had made radical revisions to Somerset's defence plans, including halting construction of forts Somerset had begun and then building posts along his own line of defence. In a move that confirmed his complete disregard for Somerset, Donkin had an argument with Somerset's son, and, waving a whip over Henry's head, placed the young man under open arrest in Simonstown.

Barry, too, had had problems with Donkin. When Barry left the colony to deal with an outbreak of cholera on the nearby island of Mauritius, Donkin decided to cut back on what seemed to him some very extravagant spending. On Barry's return she discovered he had slashed budgets for all departments, including the hospital.

When Somerset finally returned, the Cape was a powder keg. He walked in one door of Government House as Donkin walked out another. The two did not meet face to face but vented their anger in a series of notes. Donkin claimed he had "no official communication" to make to Somerset, an unusual statement from someone who had been acting governor for two years, who had seen the greatest influx of immigrants ever to land in Africa and who had made major changes to Somerset's plans. Donkin soon left the colony, but it was a bitter departure, and on his return to London he continued his attacks on Somerset. It took all of Somerset's diplomatic skill to return the Cape to the relatively peaceful state it was in before he left. Barry and Somerset's son, Henry, were particularly grateful for Somerset's renewed efforts on the Cape's behalf.

Chapter Seven

THE RUMOUR

O N JUNE 1, 1824, BARRY'S WORLD was sent reeling. Captain John Findlay, a local resident, out for an early morning stroll, noticed a poster nailed to the notice board at the corner of Heerengracht and Hour streets. Quickly he read it, rushed home, then returned. By that time the poster had disappeared, but other early risers had also seen it, and word of its contents quickly spread through town.

It is not known who brought the news to Barry and Somerset, but it must have been a difficult task. The poster suggested an unnatural relationship between the two men. A number of local merchants, who were also scandalized by the suggestion, joined Barry and Somerset to raise a fourteen-thousand rixdollar reward for anyone who could name the perpetrator.

Strong circumstantial evidence suggested William Edwards was responsible. He had the motive. He held a grudge against Somerset. He had the ability and the resources, but he was in jail at the time of the incident. Somerset suspected Edwards had made the poster and hired someone to put it up for him but could not prove this.

Later, Edwards admitted that it had indeed been his handiwork and offered Somerset an apology. But an apology could never undo the harm Edwards had caused. Barry knew she had to maintain an arm's length relationship with Somerset from then on. She felt betrayed and angered that such a good friendship could be twisted and tainted. Of course, the allegations were preposterous, and she could easily have disproved them by revealing herself as a woman. Before Lord Charles had remarried, she had even allowed herself to consider the possibility of becoming the second Lady Somerset. The idea was not beyond the realm of possibility. They were good friends. They enjoyed each other's company. She got along well with Somerset's children. With Somerset as a husband she would have a highly ranked protector and a comfortable life. There would have been a flurry of gossip when she announced her sex, but that would die down eventually. And in the distant reach of the Cape colony she might even have been able to continue her medical practice, this time unhampered by a disguise. She had already proven her abilities. But Somerset had remarried, and for Barry to reveal her disguise now would mean risking her career. This she could not bring herself to do.

Somerset would never learn Barry's true gender. He had enjoyed her company and appreciated her many abilities. He had taken her into his home and treated her like a member of the family. The spurt of gossip set in action by the scurrilous placard was a harsh warning to Barry. Whether Somerset realized it or not, it affected their relationship ever after. As long as she continued her present role, Barry could never allow herself to become closely involved with another person. She could never be friendly with a young woman. That way lay disaster. Nor could she allow herself to become close to any of the young men in the colony. She knew now what the gossips might say about that.

It was a bitter moment. Even the child she had so recently delivered was a poignant reminder of one more pleasure she must deny herself. She would never experience motherhood, the loving relationship of marriage, the special closeness of her own family or the delight of watching her children grow.

Barry threw herself into her work with increasing fury,

tightening her grip on each of the departments assigned to her and apparently giving no thought to the feelings of those with whom she worked.

Lord Charles continued to support Barry, but even his approval wasn't enough to smooth the many feathers she ruffled. Perhaps she could have been more successful had she taken the time to explain her actions to others as she may have explained them to Somerset. But she did not. If something needed changing, it was to be changed instantly. She cared not a fig for traditions or customs. Her fiery temper and tactless manner, along with her refusal to listen to other points of view, led to many quarrels and left a growing trail of enemies behind her.

Barry was aware of the problem, but apologizing, explaining, deferring—these could all be taken as signs of weakness. And, she feared, unless she appeared invulnerable, questions about her femininity or her lack of masculine boldness might lead to her unmasking.

In an effort to reinforce her identity, she exaggerated masculine traits and unwittingly made herself into a comic figure. Her costumes became more outlandish. Even her most sedate outfits looked somehow wrong. Swords, for example, were considered a part of male accoutrement, normally worn only on dress or ceremonial occasions. Barry, however, wore a full-length sword as part of her everyday costume. The effect was even more comical because it dangled around her ankles, often threatening to trip her.

Then there was the way she walked. She swaggered along on her built-up boots, trying to appear ready to challenge anyone who crossed her path. Her balance was affected by the boots, and further emphasized her feminine gait. She always cradled Psyche in the crook of one arm as she strode along, and onlookers couldn't help but notice her unusual combination of bravado and tenderness. When she overheard their whispered comments, she decided not to walk along the roads and streets. Thereafter, she and Psyche rode her pony wherever and whenever possible.

Along with trying to look as masculine as she could, Barry also tried to sound as masculine as she could, at times making crude remarks because she thought it was a mannish thing to do. One such incident quickly blew into a full-fledged storm. While talking to the governor's *aide-de-camp*, Josias Cleote, Barry made highly sexist remarks about a woman who had called on the governor and then added a crude suggestion about the governor's behaviour towards women.

"That is a scurrilous and cowardly thing to say about Lord Charles," Cleote fumed. He backed up his statement by suddenly advancing on Barry and stretching out his hand. "There," he said. "I am pulling your long ugly nose. What do you have to say to that?"

Barry felt she had no recourse. She challenged Cleote to a duel. The two fought with pistols. Luckily neither was a very good shot, and both emerged unscathed. In later years they became good friends and remained so as long as they lived. But Barry never seemed to learn from past mistakes. She was always shocking and upsetting those around her. Even her medical procedures seemed outrageous to her colleagues. At the time, night air was considered dangerous. Sick people were protected not just from night air but from fresh air as well. But Barry believed fresh air was critical. Her entry into a sickroom was dramatic.

"Open those windows," she ordered, sending housemaids scurrying towards the casements. Often she helped the process along by tearing the curtains from their hangers to ensure the flow of fresh air into the room.

"Throw out these pills," she demanded, scooping up pills, potions and whatever other concoctions the patient was taking.

"Tell the cook to stop making these messes," she continued, curling her lip at the delicacies on a lunch tray.

Only then did she begin to treat patients, starting them on a healthy diet of fruits and vegetables with perhaps a very small portion of meat or a cooked egg accompanied by lots of liquids.

If there was an infection she often ordered wine. "Never mind smiling," she told the startled patient. "It isn't for you. It's for the infection," she said as she bathed the infection in Cape wine. The alcohol acted as a disinfectant and often helped healing. "I want you to bathe in the ocean as well," she added. The combination of sunshine and saltwater had powerful germ-killing properties, but most people, confused by superstitions and generations of misinformation, didn't understand the reasons for her actions. Even some of her colleagues didn't seem to understand much about germs, especially older doctors who had not kept up with new discoveries.

However unorthodox her treatments seemed, most of her patients recovered, and her fame had spread throughout the colony. She was one of the first Cape physicians to use the stethoscope, which was developed by Laennec in Paris in 1813. Just as Laennec said, listening to the heart and lungs of her patients made it easier to evaluate some illnesses and to monitor recoveries. To Barry's patients the stethoscope and other new devices bordered on witchcraft.

In 1820 Barry performed an operation that must have confirmed their suspicions. The wife of Thomas Munnik, a wealthy Cape snuff maker, was expecting a child. Complications during labour brought Mrs. Munnik to the point of death. With the midwife unable to help, Thomas Munnik galloped to Dr. Barry's quarters and pleaded with her to save his wife. Barry responded. A quick examination revealed that the baby was too large to be born in the usual manner.

Dr. James Hamilton, one of Barry's professors at the University of Edinburgh, had performed two Caesarean operations. Neither was successful, but Hamilton had described the process carefully for his students. It was a little-known and seldom-used option. Instead most doctors gave the father a choice. Using less drastic procedures they could attempt to save the mother or save the child. But not both.

Barry believed a Caesarean might allow her to save both. Alternatively she could lose both. There were no general anaesthetics, and the operation would be painful. Quickly she outlined the procedure to Munnik. "If you agree, I will do my best," Barry promised.

Munnik looked at his wife, weakened, stained with sweat and gasping for breath. He took a moment for prayer before he turned to Barry. "Do it," he said. "And may God hold your hand."

Barry operated at once. Munnik's wife lived, as did her healthy baby boy. The Munnik case is believed to be only the second successful Caesarean in medical history. It would be many years later, in 1833, before a successful Caesarean was performed in England.

"Thank-you," Thomas Munnik said. "Thank-you from the bottom of my heart. You don't yet have a son. May I give our little boy your name?"

Flattered, Barry agreed. James Barry Munnik grew up to become town clerk in the township of Wynberg. His son, also named James Barry Munnik, became godfather to another little boy named James Barry Munnik Hertzog. That baby grew up to be prime minister of South Africa.

Barry had many medical triumphs at the Cape. Her colleagues recognized her abilities and called on her for consultation in difficult cases, but her abrasive manner still created problems, and her temper grew more and more out of control. The next lightning rod was the unregulated sale of patent medicines and drugs at the Cape.

Patent medicines were everywhere. There were no controls on their production or sale. People could buy them and use them for whatever purpose they wished. The ingredients might be little more than flavoured water with a few drops of colouring added, or they could be a lethal mixture of alcohol, arsenic, codeine or opium derivatives.

"People are dying out there because of these medicines," she raged as she outlined the Cape's unregulated drug business to Somerset. "I believe the hawkers and peddlers kill more people than the diseases these medicines are supposed to cure. Drugs should only be sold by people specially trained in their uses and preparation," Barry insisted. "But these medicines are sold like penny candies." There had been several instances of parents, who knew no better, giving adult dosages to young children with fatal results. These were heartbreaking needless deaths.

It seemed Barry was in a no-win situation. The drug sellers and importers fought against restrictions or controls. The purchasers defended their right to choose their own medicines. All sides flooded the office of the chief justice with petitions and arguments. Finally he reached a decision: the act would remain exactly as it was.

Barry was not through fighting, though. As colonial medical inspector, one of her responsibilities was examining all candidates for apothecary* licences. When it suited her purposes, Barry broke rules without a thought. Though she had broken rules about women attending university, becoming a doctor and joining the army, she was a stickler for her own rules and expected others to follow them to the letter. She picked an unlikely subject to make her point.

Charles Frederick Liesching, a Cape resident, applied for a licence to become an apothecary. He had been a pharmacist's apprentice for five years and had spent another five years as acting partner in the pharmacy, helping mix and dispense

*pharmacist

drugs under the supervision of his licenced partner. There was no school of pharmacy in South Africa, and it would be a hardship for Liesching to travel to Europe, where he would have to support himself during the time it took to earn a diploma in pharmacy. He already had ten years of study and training. His advisers assured him the licence was just a formality.

Barry, however, refused to consider his application. Late one evening, at the governor's residence, she reviewed the situation once again. "Liesching has no professional education or documents," she said. "Testing him would set a precedent for anyone to apply for a licence. Even Shaka Zulu's old witch doctors out in the hill could apply for a licence." She shook her head resolutely. "No, I cannot allow it."

"Why don't you at least examine the man?" Somerset asked. "If he fails the test that will be the end of it."

But Barry refused.

The case dragged on for over a year with feelings on each side becoming more and more bitter. Finally Barry asked to be relieved of the duty of examining Liesching and that a medical board be convened to look into the question. They awarded the licence. Liesching's friends saw the issue as right against wrong with Dr. Barry being wrong. Once again she made enemies. Soon she would make more.

Since her arrival at the Cape, Barry had been concerned by conditions in the Tronk, as the local jail was known. Men, women and children lived together in a common cell with no regard for privacy or for protecting the smaller and weaker prisoners. The prison was filthy, the food almost inedible and conditions absolutely wretched. Sadistic guards used the slightest excuse to beat prisoners.

On one visit to the Tronk, Barry discovered Jacob Elliott, a prisoner, lying on the floor with an untreated broken leg. Incensed, she marched into the governor's office and reported the offence. "He was without a bed or pillows," she raged. "His blankets were dirty in the extreme, and he was without a single comfort."

Then she discovered another prisoner, this one in solitary confinement. Like Elliot he had a broken leg. His other leg was chained to the wall. Barry sent both men to hospital and denounced prison officials for their negligence. Prison administrators responded quickly. They charged Barry with making slurs against their characters, and she was summoned before the court to defend herself.

Barry flew into a rage. She grabbed the summons from the messenger's hand, tore it into a dozen pieces and threw them into his hat. "There," she fumed. "Take that back to your masters."

Barry was found guilty of the charges and sentenced to one month in jail. "I should cut off their ears," she fumed. It was Barry's favourite expression. If she acted every time she was annoyed, most of the officials in Cape Town would have been earless. Instead of attacking the judge's ears, however, she appealed to her friend, the governor. Lord Charles set aside the sentence.

Barry seemed to move from one extreme to the other. She made many enemies over the Liesching licence and more over the Tronk affair. Then she did something that drew praise and admiration from the residents of the colony. An epidemic of typhus broke out in one of the surrounding districts. Typhus can sweep through a village, striking down victims in unpredictable patterns and with blinding speed. A person who is healthy one day can be dead two days later. Typhus begins with a fever, which leads to delirium. If telltale purple spots erupt it usually sounds the death knell for the victim.

Cape Town residents watched fearfully, afraid the outbreak would spread to their neighbourhoods. Barry knew there were too many victims for her to treat. She did not have enough trained staff to send to the district, and there was little that could be done once the disease took hold. Prevention was her only weapon.

She persuaded a printer to help her with an unusual plan. She drew up a poster containing information on preventing the disease from spreading and on caring for those already afflicted. Barry sent the posters to officials in the surrounding areas. "Paste these on walls, posts and fences," she instructed. "Make sure the instructions are followed to the letter." Strict cleanliness was essential. Every home had to be cleared of rats and mice. Lice had to be eradicated, even if it meant shaving heads and burning clothing. The Cape breathed a sigh of relief as the epidemic abated and life returned to normal. For at least a brief period, Barry was a hero.

Then Cape residents discovered something more interesting than the antics of the little doctor. It erupted in politics. A few years earlier more than four thousand immigrants had arrived from England. They had changed the character of the population from mixed Dutch and English to predominantly English. Members of this new group were unhappy about the way in which the governor ruled the colony. "There is no democracy or representation," they grumbled. Somerset could not understand their complaints. The colony was governed the way all British colonies were governed, and he saw no reason to change.

When the new immigrants gathered to talk about the problem, their meetings were interrupted and they were sent back to their homes. Then Somerset invoked an old law. All meetings held without his sanction were declared illegal. When the newspapers tried to write about the situation, they discovered the governor had some rules for them as well. Before they could publish their papers, they had to promise not to print anything about controversial issues. Thomas Pringle, publisher of the *South African Journal,* stopped publishing his paper rather than make that promise.

Unhappy settlers sent letters and petitions to England, flooding the Home Office, the House of Commons and the King's Council with pages of complaints. A royal commission met in 1825 and after long discussion told Somerset he must govern with the assistance of a council. Later that year, the Colonial Office divided the Cape into two administrative units. Lord Charles would continue to govern in the western half. It effectively marked the end of his career.

The 1820s were turbulent years for the colony. Early in the decade blight wiped out two successive wheat harvests, sending bread prices skyrocketing. New customs charges were levied on wool exported from the Cape, devastating the sheep farmers. Heavy storms in the western Cape flooded crops, drowned cattle and caused severe damage to buildings, roads and bridges. Then the colony was hit by an economic ruling. London declared that British silver was to be the colony's legal tender. The exchange was set at the rate of one shilling sixpence for each rixdollar. The rate previously had been four shillings per rixdollar. The abrupt devaluation sent the Cape's economy reeling.

In England, a financial crisis in 1825 set off a tide of bankruptcies when sixty-five banks closed their doors, forcing merchants to cancel orders. Those at the Cape, dependent on bankers and merchants in England, were hit even harder.

During these years there was no time for dissension. Cape residents, including Barry, set aside differences and worked to restore the colony. When life began to return to normal, Barry once again had time to brood over slights and perceived injustices. Her thoughts returned to the jail sentence. Somerset had set it aside, but in her eyes that didn't make it right. It should not have been given at all. Her honour had been challenged.

Barry asked for a royal commission to clear her name. Sir Richard Plaskett, newly appointed to fill the position left by Somerset, refused Barry's request. At the same time Cape officials decided they had had enough of her ongoing challenges to their authority.

It was a difficult situation. No one had ever complained about the conduct of Barry's department. She was an excellent surgeon and an efficient administrator. But an old piece of legislation gave Cape officials the opportunity they sought. According to the document, "The Colonial Medical Department should not be in the hands of any one person, but should be conducted by a committee." The rule was brought to Barry's attention. Barry had many responsibilities, both civil and military. She welcomed the idea of a committee to help run the medical department. Naturally she assumed she would head the committee. Then Sir Richard struck. He called her into his office to name the members of the committee.

"You will, of course, be a member," he said.

Barry smiled.

However, he continued, she would be the most junior member. As such she would have the least influence on its decisions. Now it was Sir Richard's turn to smile.

Once again Barry turned to her friend, the governor. This time he could not help her. The new committee formed and offered Barry the position of junior member. She refused. To make her point she then resigned from each of the positions she held at the Cape.

It was a time for changes all around. Lord Charles returned to England to attend a hearing in London dealing with complaints made by the immigrants. He was cleared of all charges and returned to the Cape "without a stain upon his character." But too much had happened. Despite his enormous popularity in the colony (and Secretary of the Council Dudley Perceval reported that he was the most popular man in the colony despite what his political enemies in London said) Somerset resigned. He and his family, which by this time included another daughter and a son, would return to England. Unhappily he had to leave his son, Henry, and his grandchildren at the Cape. He would never see them again.

On March 5, 1826, to the accompaniment of a nineteen-gun salute, Lord Charles and his family were escorted to the government barge, which was steered by Deputy Port Captain Pedder, accompanied by Lieutenant Colonel and Lady Fitzroy, Lady C. Bell, Lieutenant Rundell, Mr. C. Blair and James Barry. Two additional boats carried the remaining dignitaries, forming an escort. The Somersets boarded the *Atlas* standing by in the harbour and ready to leave for England. It was an emotional send off. Later that evening, Barry held onto Psyche, the only real companion left to her. "I'm going to miss them," she told the pup. "They've been like family."

Barry continued her work at the Cape. On November 22, 1827, she was promoted from colonial medical inspector to staff surgeon to the forces. The promotion surprised Barry. She thought her career had been shattered, but it appears the Home Office discounted much of what had happened and recognized her achievements. In 1828 she left for a new posting on the island of Mauritius.

When Barry left Cape Town she probably never realized just how much she had accomplished in her fight against cruelty and injustice in the Cape. The royal commission Barry had requested presented a series of recommendations based largely on her complaints. These led to changes in the Cape's prison, hospital and judicial systems. Barry was not there to see these changes, but through them she left a deeper mark on the colony than she ever suspected.

Barry set sail for Mauritius, looking forward to a clean slate in her new posting. She had no idea that two of her most serious challenges lay directly ahead of her.

Chapter Eight

THE CHALLENGE

THE STATE OF MAURITIUS is made up of a cluster of islands in the Western Indian Ocean about two thousand miles from Cape Town, to the northeast of the Reunion Islands, off Madagascar. The capital city of Port Louis is on the largest island, also called Mauritius. The twin islands of Andrigues and Agelaga are the next most populated, followed by a group of smaller islands that make up the De Cargados Carajos Achipelago. Although Mauritius exported sugar, tea, tobacco and ebony, its major importance was as a way station for ships en route to India and the Far East.

Barry left Cape Town on October 8, 1828, and took up her duties immediately on arrival at Port Louis. She knew Mauritius from previous visits and lost little time settling in. She was blissfully unaware that a serious threat to her disguise was on the horizon.

A Mr. and Mrs. Fenton, travelling from India to New South Wales, Australia, made an unscheduled stop at Mauritius. Mrs. Fenton was in the late stages of pregnancy. She was too uncomfortable to face the remainder of her journey and worried about having her baby aboard ship with only a ship's doctor to care for her. The Fentons decided it would be safer for her to disembark at Mauritius and wait there for the arrival of the baby.

Mr. Fenton made arrangements for his wife to stay at Government House, hired a doctor to care for her and then resumed his journey. She planned to join him in Australia as soon as she and the baby were able to travel.

Mrs. Fenton was intrigued to learn that Dr. Barry was on the island and remembered a strange story she had heard. Mrs. Fenton's informant was a nurse who had lived and worked in Cape Town for several years before moving to Calcutta. Dr. Barry had been in charge of many of her patients.

"One night," she'd told Mrs. Fenton, "one of my patients took a turn for the worse. He needed help immediately, so I sent someone to Dr. Barry's quarters to wake him up and ask him to come quickly."

The nurse waited for what seemed a long period until, desperate for help, she left her patient, ran to Barry's quarters and rushed in without knocking.

"At that moment," she said, lowering her voice for effect, "Dr. Barry had thrown off his nightgown and stood naked before me!"

The nurse paused in her story. She was accustomed to seeing nude bodies, she explained. It was not that which shocked her. When she looked at the doctor, it was instantly apparent that Dr. Barry was not a man.

"As a nurse and as a woman, I swear that Dr. Barry was a female," she avowed.

The doctor dismissed her immediately and never again allowed her to care for his patients. Clearly, the nurse said, he was afraid she might reveal his secret. Not long after, the nurse left Cape Town for Calcutta, where she met Mrs. Fenton.

Mrs. Fenton was amused by the tale, but because she never expected to meet the mysterious doctor in person, she forgot about it. Now, through a quirk of fate, she had a chance to meet Dr. Barry face to face.

Mrs. Fenton's baby was born soon after her arrival. The civilian doctor her husband had hired was unable to attend the delivery. Instead she was cared for by one of the doctors under Barry's command. During the weeks following baby Flora's birth, Mrs. Fenton struck up a friendship with Dr. Barry, and putting the baby in a carrying basket, joined Barry on daily walks.

She never mentioned the nurse's story to Barry. She did not gossip about it at the time, but she did write the story in her diary, which was published many years later, after Barry's death. "There is," she wrote, "something extraordinary about this same Dr. Barry." She made no further comment and never revealed exactly what it was that she found so extraordinary.

Mrs. Fenton's recovery was uncomplicated, and before long she was able to travel. She left for New South Wales to rejoin her husband, keeping the mysterious tale to herself.

Soon after, a ship arrived bearing bad news for Barry. The first was word of the death of her patron, the Earl of Buchan. He was eighty-seven years old when he died, and he had enjoyed a full and active life. He had no legal heirs, so his title went to a nephew. It was impossible for Barry to attend Buchan's funeral, held at Dryburgh in Edinburgh on April 25, 1829, but in her own way she mourned his passing. Now there was no one left with whom to share her secret.

The other news, even more devastating, was from Lord Somerset's brother, Lord Fitzroy Somerset. Lord Charles was seriously ill. Barry did not hesitate. In August 1829 she took unofficial leave, boarding the next ship bound for England. On December 13 she reported to the director-general of the medical department in London.

Barry was willing to put her career on the line for her friend, despite the knowledge that it would leave a black mark on an otherwise blemish-free record. Perhaps she hoped she might escape punishment because Somerset's brother, Fitzroy, was military secretary.

She remained with Lord Charles for fourteen months.

Under her care Somerset rallied to the point where he was once again able to enjoy horseback riding and to accept an appointment as colonel of the Thirty-Third Regiment of Foot. Despite Barry's best efforts, however, Somerset died suddenly on Sunday, February 20, 1831. Barry joined her friend's grief-stricken family at the funeral. She felt Somerset's loss deeply and maintained a close relationship with his family over the years.

During her time in London, Barry had visited specialists and read the latest medical literature, trying to discover ways to help Lord Charles. At the time the medical world was buzzing with the exciting discovery made by James Simpson, a Scottish physician and professor at her Alma Mater, the University of Edinburgh. Simpson had developed a compound that could put people into an artificial sleep.

"What a blessing," Barry commented when she first learned of the discovery. Over the years she had performed major surgery on patients who were wide awake. She knew that fear, tension and shock made the operations harder on the patient and more difficult for the surgeon. During her stay in London, she learned as much about the new compound as she could.

Two months after Lord Charles' death, Barry left London for her next posting, this time as staff surgeon with the Third West Indian Regiment in the garrison of Jamaica.

Jamaica, then as now, was a beautiful island. Warm breezes, tropical plants and flowers, and the clear sparkling waters of the surrounding ocean made an idyllic setting. But for all its beauty, Jamaica was not a pleasant place. It was known throughout the military world as a fever post—an unhealthy place where fevers of many sorts threatened the lives of soldiers and civilians.

Soon after Barry arrived, a serious outbreak of yellow fever, or Yellow Jack, swept through the garrison. Barry was alerted when first a trickle and then a flood of troopers appeared at the infirmary complaining of fever and headaches. Patients followed a predictable course. On the second day, pain spread, causing backaches and aching muscles. The gums bled and the tongue turned bright red, like a strawberry. By the third day temperatures soared, reaching a hundred and four degrees Fahrenheit or more. On the fourth day there was a period of remission, which normally lasted two days. The fever dropped, nausea cleared up, headaches eased and patients felt much better. This was, however, the most dangerous point because many patients considered themselves cured and returned to their daily routine.

"Don't let them out of bed," Barry instructed the orderlies.

"But they say they're all better," the men replied.

"I don't care what they say. They are not," Barry answered grimly. Soon her predictions were borne out. The brief period of remission ended, and the fever returned, this time attacking the liver. During this phase victims suffered the severe jaundice, or yellowing, which gives the fever its name, and nausea returned, but their vomit was black. The disease killed fifty percent of its victims. Complications were responsible for additional deaths.

Even today strict cleanliness, bed rest and hydration are important in the treatment of yellow fever. In Barry's day they were the only weapons available. It was a frightening disease that struck quickly, spread like wildfire and created panic in the population.

There was one positive note, and Barry was quick to take advantage of it. Those who survived an attack of Yellow Jack were immune thereafter. Wherever possible she recruited those who were immune to help care for new victims.

Barry put preventive measures in place even as she dealt with outbreaks of the disease. "The men are to use the mosquito nets they have been issued," she instructed. "And warn them I shall be inspecting to make sure the nets are in good repair."

Troopers often didn't bother with the mosquito nets. They felt nets were a nuisance, and mending the fragile material was regarded as women's work. But Barry didn't care what they thought of her orders as long as they were carried out. Grudgingly the men complied. Afterwards, when Barry was alone with Psyche, she'd mutter, "I don't care what the men think of my orders. And I don't care what it takes to make them carry out those orders." The little dog cocked his head to one side, listening carefully.

Suddenly Barry laughed. "I wish they would pay as much attention to me as you do."

More regulations followed. "Drinking water must be taken from a safe source," she announced. "It must be far enough from camp to avoid contamination. And all able-bodied men are responsible for keeping barracks areas clean." Grumbling reached a new high, but Barry enforced her rules.

After successfully containing several outbreaks of yellow fever, Barry began hearing stories about slave rebellions and uprisings among the Jamaican blacks. The white settlers on the island were vastly outnumbered, but it was they who held positions of responsibility and authority and they who controlled the wealth. The island had been a powder keg for many years. The unrest had begun in 1807 when Britain abolished the slave trade. Blacks in Jamaica assumed this meant emancipation for them. When they were not freed, they believed the landowners were holding them illegally. From 1807 to 1831, slaves staged a series of uprisings, each larger than the last and each followed by harsh repressive measures. The Great Christmas Rising of 1831 was the largest uprising and played a critical part in Jamaica's move towards independence, although this was many years in the future.

During the uprising, Barry was trapped in a garrison on

the far side of the island, where she was making one of her routine visits. Commanding officers had been killed or captured. As the ranking officer it was her responsibility to direct the troops in defending the fort. She performed to the best of her ability, becoming one of the few medical officers in British army history to take a leading role in battle.

Barry knew little of military strategy, and in her heart she sympathized with the insurgents. But she had to protect the soldiers left in the fort. Surrender would have been an invitation to swift and terrible retaliation. The garrison rallied, the attackers were beaten off and soon the uprising ended.

There were few casualties among the soldiers, but the event had compromised her morally. It was a sad victory. Like her Uncle James, and her mentors Buchan and Miranda, Barry was opposed to slavery. It was an institution that degraded both the slaves and those who used them. In many of her postings, however, slavery was common. Fieldworkers and house servants were often slaves.

"I will not have a slave in my household," Barry announced to the amusement of her friends. But she was adamant. Instead she hired a freeman and paid him regular wages. It set a good example and sent a strong message.

Life returned to normal in Jamaica, and Barry continued her hospital routines, including her ongoing battle to improve the men's diets, clean up camp areas and provide a safe water supply. Anxiously she combed medical journals, looking for references to back her demands.

"If they accuse me of pampering the soldiers one more time, I shall cut off their ears," she muttered as she searched for information to convince the commanding officer that good nutrition was essential. "The conditions of the troops are bad enough without someone blathering about mollycoddling every time I try to improve things."

Medical journals were an important part of her continuing

struggle to keep up with the latest information and newest procedures in medicine. From time to time they also brought news of former colleagues. Each issue was precious, and she read each from cover to cover.

An 1833 journal carried a small item about McGill University in the Canadian colony of Lower Canada. It had just awarded its first medical degree to William Leslie Logan. It was fitting that the first degree was awarded to a son of Scotland. The university's own name honoured another Scot, James McGill.

McGill made his start as a Montreal fur trader, later went into politics and became a very wealthy man. Along with his other interests he had been commanding officer of a Montreal militia battalion. McGill's battalion had been in charge of defending Montreal against American invasion in 1812.

Barry had heard many stories about Canada although she had never been there. "I'm told it's a beautiful country," she said, absently stroking Psyche's ears. "But I've also heard it's very cold—even colder than England. I think I'd rather stay here."

Barry's tour of duty in Jamaica was short. She returned to England for home leave in 1835 and once again enjoyed the company of Lady Somerset and her family. In 1836 she was given another promotion and a new posting. She was sent to the island of St. Helena as principal medical officer.

Prior to Barry's arrival, Charles Darwin, whose theories of evolution threw the scientific and religious communities into turmoil, had stopped at St. Helena aboard his famous ship, the *Beagle*. While there he investigated the curious flora and fauna of the island. St. Helena's isolation in the south Atlantic Ocean, like the isolation of the Galapagos Archipelago in the Pacific, helped him trace the evolution of many varieties of plants and animals. Like many others, Darwin had paused to visit Napoleon's last resting place.

St. Helena had been owned for many years by the East

India Company. It was occupied by Britain in 1815 and formally transferred to His Majesty's Government in 1833. The island was vitally important as a way station for sailing ships travelling between Britain and Cape Town or the Cape of Good Hope. It was surprisingly small, just ten by six miles, but sailing ships used the anchorage as the one safe haven accessible to them along the coastline. Today powerboats can take advantage of over forty little bays and coves, but in Barry's day winds and tides made these impractical for sailing ships. Indeed, winds and water currents were major problems for any ocean travel. Prevailing winds could sweep a ship far off its course, while major currents had the same effect on ships as the jet stream does on airplanes: it could help or hinder, depending upon the direction of travel. And because ships were powered entirely by sail, lack of wind was equally problematic. Captains often tried to outguess the weather, but it was difficult to know whether to take the long way around to ensure fair winds or risk a shorter crossing with the possibility of no wind.

The trip from Australia or Cape Town to England could take many months in adverse conditions. Way stations such as St. Helena provided respite from the long journey, and captains could repair damaged vessels, take on fresh water and reprovision their ships.

Sailors approaching St. Helena first see a puff of cloud on the horizon. Then as they draw closer, it changes to a small hump that looks like the back of a whale. Then the hump becomes a row of forbidding cliffs. The anchorage on St. Helena led to the establishment of the island's only town, Jamestown, which was set in a deep ravine. The difference in altitude between Jamestown at sea level and the plateau above town was dramatic. While groves of olive and lemon trees, giant fuschia plants and other verdant growth ranged over the plateau, vegetation in Jamestown was much more sparse and desert-like. St. Helena is a natural fortress, which is the reason the British government chose the island as the site of Napoleon's exile. Barry, like most visitors, was familiar with the story of Napoleon's banishment to St. Helena and of the minicourt he established here. A few of the buildings he had occupied still remained when Barry arrived. His tomb was intact with its multiple layers of coffins and barriers to protect it from grave robbers. It was in danger both from supporters, who wanted to move it to a more honourable site, and detractors, who wanted to desecrate his resting place.

Barry's first sight of the island had been many years earlier as a young doctor on the way to her first overseas posting at Cape Town. At that time security had been so strict that no one was allowed to disembark except for the ship's captain and the crew members responsible for refilling the ship's water barrels. This time there were no such restrictions. Napoleon was long dead, and the island was once again simply a way station and watering stop.

Thoughts of Napoleon evoked other memories for Barry. The French general had been both a friend and colleague to General Miranda and had mentioned him in his writings. The two had corresponded during the French Revolution and in the years that followed. Barry's fondness for Miranda brought on a flood of memories.

"So much has happened since then," she murmured to Psyche as she leaned against the ship's rail, watching the island draw nearer. "At least I was able to prove him right: given the proper training, women can be admirable surgeons."

And yet it had been a lonely life. Her closest companion was still Psyche, who continued to share her secrets. She clutched the little dog to her chest and scratched behind its ears.

Once disembarked, Barry found she was again facing a crisis. The island was battling an epidemic of dysentery. Again she found the same dismal and dirty conditions. "Don't these people ever learn!" she fumed. "How many times in how many places have I told commanding officers that sanitation must be improved to prevent this sort of thing. And if the men are to keep their health, their diets must be improved as well. They cannot live in filth and expect to be healthy. There is no excuse for allowing sewage near a water source. Nor is there any excuse here for requiring soldiers to live on bread and meat alone."

Once again Barry flew into action, issuing streams of orders. Build proper latrines. Keep them away from the water supply. Make everyone wash their hands before they touch food. Everyone. Cooks, helpers and soldiers alike. Screen all windows and keep flies away from the food. Add fresh fruits and vegetables to the menu.

Once the epidemic was under control she took a long look at conditions in the hospital. She was not happy with what she found. "Why are male attendants caring for female patients?" she demanded.

"Why not?" the authorities replied. "Male attendants have always cared for female patients. Why shouldn't they?"

Barry heard horrifying stories of abuses, and these, combined with her own sensitivity, confirmed to her that it was wrong to have male attendants in female wards. But her complaints were ignored. Once again she muttered her favourite threat, which would have left yet another group of officials earless. Action was required, so Barry hired a local black woman to act as matron in the female wards.

"This time Barry has gone too far," officials in the civil department complained. "We are responsible for staffing the hospital, not Barry. His eternal interference has got to stop."

They took their complaints to Governor Middlemore, who had a fearsome reputation on the island for being both bad mannered and discourteous. He was not the sort of person to put up with what he regarded as meddling, and in his view that was precisely what Barry was doing. It was the first of many complaints he received about Barry.

The governor and Barry's commanding officer were outraged by her disregard for protocol—that rigid code of procedures that governed military, diplomatic and social events. Barry was hauled before the garrison's officers for the "flagrant breach of discipline." This time, they said, she had "knowingly gone over the head of her commanding officer." She was held for court martial.

After hearing her defence the military court acquitted her and fully endorsed her recommendations regarding female patients in the Civil Hospital. The court vindicated her, but it did nothing to endear her to Middlemore.

Encouraged by her success, Barry once again began badgering authorities to make improvements in the hospital wards and, in particular, in the food provided for patients in the hospital. In her view it was completely inadequate and totally inappropriate for invalids and convalescents. She wrote report after report on the situation, making a long series of recommendations to the authorities.

Finally her temper snapped. "If these local louts won't listen to me, I'll write to someone who can make them pay attention," she muttered to Psyche.

That evening she sharpened her quill pen, drafted a letter to the secretary of state and the War Office in London, corrected it and then made a final copy. It was sent on the next ship. Then, as she waited for instructions from the secretary of state, she ordered the assistant commissary general of St. Helena to furnish patients with the kinds of food they needed.

Barry knew that according to military rules, all recommendations and all correspondence must go through established channels of communication. That was standard procedure. But once again Barry felt her patients' needs carried more weight than military protocol. Rules and regulations should not apply to her if they interfered with what she saw as her duty. Once again she managed to incur the wrath of her commanding officer.

Despite Barry's fiery temper and her disregard for protocol, she was very kind to her patients. Many commented that she had "hands like a woman," so gentle was her touch and so delicate her surgery. She was deeply concerned about the welfare of patients, both soldiers and civilians, placed in her care.

At the same time, she had nothing but contempt for those in positions of authority who did not understand what she was trying to accomplish. She fought, argued, bickered, nagged and made life miserable for them. If one approach failed, she tried another. Her gadfly persistence was a continuing challenge—and a continuing annoyance. Often her actions made officials so angry they became blind to the rationale behind her complaints.

In April 1838 Barry finally went too far. On Middlemore's orders she was placed under arrest and sent to London. This time she could not escape discipline. She was reduced in rank and posted back to the West Indies.

It was little consolation to know that Middlemore's actions caused as much grief to other members of the Jamestown community as they had to her. For various reasons from 1836–1838, entire families and more than 110 single persons—a significant part of the island's small population—left St. Helena and emigrated to the Cape of Good Hope. For these emigrants it was aptly named. They hoped to find a more congenial life there, away from Middlemore's rudeness and tyranny.

Chapter Nine

THE NIGHTINGALE
ENCOUNTER

FOLLOWING HER ARREST IN ST. HELENA, Barry had been demoted to staff surgeon and, on November 24, 1838, sent to the West Indies. The demotion was a tremendous blow to her pride, and conditions in the West Indies were extremely difficult. The islands were small, but they were numerous and covered a huge area. Just travelling from Antigua to the Windward and Leeward Islands took much of her time. The area was full of fever, and Barry knew hers was not an easy posting. Troopers were struck down with remittent fever, malaria and yellow fever. In addition, there were frequent outbreaks of dysentery and diseases that killed the soldiers or left them weak, helpless and susceptible to other ailments.

Over the next few years, Barry worked tirelessly to reduce the terrible toll taken by these illnesses. She travelled endlessly between the garrisons spread across the far-flung stations. Everywhere she went she repeated her doctrine of cleanliness: Wash the men. Wash the bedding. Wash the wards. Wash the hands. Clean up the barracks. Clean up the water supply. Clean up the kitchens. Improve the diet.

In her quarters she grumbled to Psyche. "Maybe I could train a parrot to repeat those words. I've said them so many times over the past twenty-five years you'd think everyone would be tired of hearing them." Psyche cocked her head to one side and wagged her tail. Despite Barry's efforts the basic rules of sanitation were still being ignored. "Death by fever or infection is a more present threat to these men than death in the course of battle," she sighed as she reached out a hand to pat Psyche's head.

Determinedly Barry continued her campaign, emphasizing cleanliness as she travelled from one garrison to another. By this time her reputation preceded her. She was known as a fusspot, who worried unnecessarily about things that were traditionally part of the soldier's lot.

The noncommissioned officers sneered openly at some of her instructions. "Might as well put bleedin' flowers beside the beds," the sergeants grumbled. Still, orders were orders, and no one wanted to send the doctor off into one of her tirades, which by this time were becoming legendary.

"All right, you men. Dr. Barry arrives on a tour of inspection tomorrow. I don't know why she wants to mollycoddle you lot, but I've got my orders. Clean up this camp." And it would be cleaned up, but as soon as Barry left, it slid back into its former state.

Barry's actions drew many derisive comments from the soldiers. Her appearance also left her open to barracks-room gibes. Barry was beginning to show her age. Her hair, once a shiny spun-copper red with glancing golden lights, had dimmed. Worse, from her point of view, were the streaks of white clearly visible at her temples. Her personal grooming now included dyeing her hair, but it was apparent that the henna tint she used was not her natural colour. Still, she continued to wage her battle against time.

When Barry looked in the mirror, there was little left of the girl she had once been. The henna darkened her hair to a flat, dull auburn colour. Her once milky complexion was now dry and hardened by tropical sunshine. Her blue eyes were no longer brilliant and had lost their sparkle as well. Age etched lines around her mouth and across her forehead. Her slim figure showed a slight stoop, and there was a certain stiffness in her movements. Refusing to accept the inevitable, she dropped years from her official records whenever she could.

She continued her disguise, swathing herself in various bands of cloth, flattening her breasts and filling out the shoulders of her jackets. It is difficult to imagine how uncomfortable all the binding and padding must have been in the tropical heat and humidity.

By this time she was officially somewhere around fifty-five years of age. In fact she was probably well into her sixties. Still, her surgical skills had not diminished, nor had her dedication to the welfare of soldiers.

Barry had to travel by sea to reach the different posts in her jurisdiction. Often she made the trip on small inter-island freighters. They lacked the accommodations and privacy to which she was accustomed. During one such trip she had to share her cabin with a young officer named Rogers. She used her superior rank to lay down the law on their first day at sea.

"All right, youngster. You will leave the cabin in the morning while I dress and in the evening while I get ready for bed."

She offered no explanation, but a junior officer needed none. Each morning he climbed down from the top bunk he occupied, dressed himself quickly and stepped outside the cabin. In the evening he stood outside the door until she told him he could enter.

"It seems peculiar to me," he told his friends, "but I can't argue with a senior officer. If Dr. Barry wants privacy, then Dr. Barry gets privacy."

Three years of fighting fever on the islands took its toll. At last Barry herself fell victim to yellow fever in Trinidad. As a physician she knew the seriousness of her illness. It was a difficult situation. "I dare not ask another physician for help," she acknowledged. "I shall have to do the best I can."

Her best was not good enough. The fever worsened and she became desperately ill, falling into a delirium. Surgeon-

General Sir T. Longmore and another doctor were called in to treat her. They pulled back the sheets to examine their patient.

"He's a woman!" they gasped.

At that moment, Barry regained consciousness. "You can't tell anyone," she begged, clutching weakly at Longmore's hand. "Swear to me—swear you'll never tell for as long as I live." They swore to keep her secret. Satisfied, Barry released Longmore's hand. "Thank-you," she whispered.

Her colleagues were men of honour and kept their word. For as long as Barry lived they told no one what they had learned. Not until after her death, when the secret of her sex had been revealed, did either man mention the incident.

Barry knew she had experienced a close call, and it raised frightening possibilities. "What if I die?" she asked herself. "What will happen then?"

She couldn't risk being dishonoured, and she knew the scandal that would erupt if her secret was made public. She called in a friend, Dr. O'Connell.

"I want you to make me a promise," she said.

"What kind of promise?"

"This is a last favour in case I die."

"Of course," O'Connell said. His friend was still very sick, and he didn't want to do anything to upset her.

"If I die you must not let anyone examine my body. And you must not let them dress me in my uniform for burial."

O'Connell's jaw dropped. Officers were always buried in full dress uniform. It was a tradition as old as the military.

"Promise," Barry repeated. "Sew me in a blanket and bury me in whatever garments I'm wearing at the time."

"Of course," O'Connell replied, thinking she was still in the grip of delirium from the fever. "Of course I will."

Satisfied, Barry fell back on the bed and allowed herself to sleep. Slowly she recovered from the fever, but it left her in a very frail and weakened condition. She was granted a year's sick leave to regain her strength. At the end of the year she returned to active duty. The next few years were extremely busy. She saw service in Malta, where she dealt with another epidemic of cholera, then went to the Ionian Islands and back again to Malta.

During this time the newspapers carried accounts of conditions that devastated her homeland. The staple food of one hundred thousand Irish families was the potato. Many families quite literally lived on nothing but boiled potatoes. Now the potato crop, hit by an airborne virus, was stricken by blight. Potatoes that appeared normal and healthy when harvested would turn to stinking piles of black muck within a week.

Tens of thousands starved to death. Tens of thousands more escaped, leaving Ireland to emigrate to North America, Australia, New Zealand or Canada. There were other smaller outbreaks of the potato blight in Europe, but farmers there planted mixed crops. When the European potato crop failed, there were still other foods to eat. In Ireland there were few alternatives and disaster occurred.

Barry no longer knew if she had kinfolk in Ireland, but every Irishman is a brother in times of trouble. However, as desperately as she wished otherwise, there was nothing she could do.

Barry continued to win promotions during her Mediterranean posting and rose to the rank of deputy inspector general of hospitals. In 1851 she was ordered to Corfu and was on duty there when the Crimean War broke out in 1854. She immediately volunteered to go to the Crimea. The regiment commanded by Lord Raglan, Lord Charles Somerset's younger brother, was on the front line. As always her loyalty was to the Somerset family.

"I'm sorry. There are no openings for anyone of your rank," she was told.

Barry didn't care about rank. She wanted to help. She even

offered to serve in the wards, doing the most menial work of all, if that was the only available opening.

The officials shook their heads. "It can't be done," they said.

Can't was not a word Barry accepted easily. She was determined to go to the Crimea. If she was refused an official posting, she would find some other way to go—but go she would!

Barry knew that casualties would be heavy. Battle wounds differ from the illnesses that affect an army in peacetime. A battlefield is a filthy place, and infections are a major concern. The soldiers would have only small field hospitals near the front lines. These would likely be overstressed and unable to handle the heavy volume of casualties.

At first she was stymied by bureaucrats with their thickets of rules and regulations. Every suggestion she made was rejected. Finally she realized the solution lay not in getting herself to the battle front but in bringing the soldiers to her as quickly as possible.

"We can set up a special transport to bring the wounded here to Corfu," she told the post commanders. On February 17, 1855, the troop transport ship *Dunbar* arrived with the first load of injured soldiers. Other transports followed, and soon Barry's hospital at Corfu was filled. This time Barry was ready. She had trained her doctors and orderlies and set in place rigid standards of cleanliness. The men muttered when she gave them their orders, but they followed the guidelines and procedures she established.

In most hospitals the death rate for battle casualties was eighty percent or higher. Barry's unit treated a total of 462 wounded men. Of these only 17 died. The casualty rate in Barry's hospital was a fraction of that in others. It was a remarkable record.

She fumed as she read the casualty statistics for other hospitals in her area. Even her exemplary survival rates were not enough to make other units adopt her procedures. Once again men were being killed by microbes, not by the enemy. And a heartbreakingly high number of those deaths could have been prevented. Soldier after soldier arrived at Corfu with infected pus-filled wounds, packed with stinking, germ-laden bandages. Barry began treatments by stripping the wounds of all the surgical packings and dressings, and tossing them in the fire.

"They only contain germs and breed more infection," she told the doctors in her command. She cleaned the wounds and left them open to the air. As always, she insisted on fresh air and good ventilation in her wards. Once again she met resistance. The patients and other medical personnel wanted the doors and windows closed tightly to protect against the "night mists" and "vapors" that were thought to carry infection. Barry demanded that doors and windows be open at all times.

"If we can avoid infection, nature will heal the wounds," she said. Other tools available to her were maggots that devoured dead flesh and leeches that drained blood from swollen tissues.

Barry upset hospital administrators by insisting that her patients have clean beds with frequent changes of bedding and mattresses.

"These men have already had clean sheets," one administrator protested.

Barry took him into the wards and told him to look at the sheets for himself. "Would you sleep on sheets that look and smell like these?" she asked. "They may have been clean once, but they need laundering now."

Finally the administrators gave up trying to argue with her. A small army of washerwomen was hired to boil the sheets. Another army of orderlies was set to cleaning floors and walls with buckets of water treated with carbolic acid. Both orderlies and soldiers grumbled about "wasting" alcohol by using it as a disinfectant. But her staff followed her orders and gradually became proud of the recovery rate in their hospital.

As the battle raged, Barry continued to press for a transfer to the front line. Time after time her request was denied. Somehow, she told herself, there had to be a way to circumvent all the regulations that prohibited her from joining Lord Raglan.

The answer, when it came, was dazzlingly simple. Since authorities were determined not to give her an official transfer to the Crimea, she would stop asking. Instead she would spend her vacation on the battlefield. "As long as I'm on vacation, I can go anywhere I want to," she whispered to Psyche, who yipped and wagged her tail. "There are no regulations about where I can take leave, but there might be rules about pets on the front line. You'll have to stay here with friends." Psyche flopped down at Barry's feet as if to show her disappointment at having to stay behind.

In fact, the idea was not that outlandish. At the time people did visit war zones, travelling as tourists to watch the battles. But Barry planned something far more interesting than a sightseeing trip.

Barry's application for leave was approved, so she spent the next three months working in an unofficial capacity in front line hospitals, using her surgical skills to mend the wounds of war and her medical knowledge to speed the healing process.

During her stay in the Crimea she met Florence Nightingale, but Barry had read about her in newspaper articles long before then. Privately she fumed as she read story after story about "The Lady with the Lamp" and the "Angel of the Crimea." Nightingale's campaign to improve the standards and status of nurses had caught the public's imagination. In Barry's eyes, Nightingale was only doing what should have been done years ago. But because she dressed in a crinoline and hoop skirt, she became a heroine to the journalists. They fell over themselves writing laudatory stories about her. Despite her annoyance, Barry enjoyed a private laugh. She, too, could have walked the wards in crinolines had she wished, and done so as a doctor, not a nurse.

But while the popular Florence Nightingale seemed to be handed everything she wanted, Barry had to fight to set in place the procedures she knew would reduce infections and speed soldiers' recoveries. She was so busy in the hospitals that she had no time to meet Nightingale socially. Nor did she want to. At times she wondered if she would encounter Nightingale in her wards, but that did not happen.

When the two finally met, it was on a parade ground. Nightingale was standing among a group of hospital attendants, and Barry was riding by on horseback. She did not dismount to talk to Nightingale but remained on her horse.

Barry had much to say to Nightingale and, with her usual lack of tact, decided there was no time like the present to say it. In front of other hospital attendants and soldiers who happened to be standing nearby, she began to lecture Nightingale on hospital procedures and policies, and scolded the nurse for some of her actions.

Nightingale was speechless with anger. After long months of battling authorities, she had finally earned a degree of respect from army officers. Civilian honours had been heaped upon her. She was certainly not prepared for the harangue that Barry delivered. She was livid at the rudeness of the little doctor who dared to keep her standing in the hot sun for a lecture.

In later years, when Nightingale learned Barry was a woman, her only comment was, "If it is true, Barry was one of the hardest women I have ever met."

Differences aside, Nightingale and Barry were dedicated

to the same idea. Both had high standards and each made heroic efforts to improve the care given sick and wounded soldiers. They had remarkable amounts of common sense, and they had both experienced the frustration of fighting their way through the fog of rules and regulations that surrounded the military. Each was fiercely determined to achieve her goal. In many ways they were very much alike. Under different circumstances they might have become friends and worked together towards their goals.

When Barry's leave ended she returned to Corfu but continued to search for ways to provide medical service. An opportunity soon presented itself. The 97th Regiment went into battle with no medical provisions and ninety-two men who suffered from cholera. Colonel Lockyer, the regimental commander, contacted Barry. It took the doctor only two hours to assemble and dispatch a supply of medicines for the regiment. No doubt it was accompanied by her usual list of instructions. She continued to send supplies on a weekly basis.

She also dealt with medical problems on board the *Modeste*. When numbers of sailors fell ill, Barry diagnosed a malignant fever, possibly a form of cholera, and promptly took over. "All sick men are to be brought up from below decks and placed in isolation on the main deck," she told the *Modeste's* captain. When he spluttered that there wasn't enough room for all of them, she ignored his protests. "Sling hammocks wherever you need to, but get them on deck in the fresh air."

Once the men had been moved, she ordered him to disinfect the ship. Every able-bodied man was expected to help. Mops were issued to all hands along with buckets of water and carbolic acid. "Now clean everything," she demanded. "Walls, floors—everything."

The captain thought she had gone mad, but he ordered his crew to follow her instructions. The outbreak halted.

Barry's work in Corfu ended in the spring of 1857. She went

to England for a well-deserved leave, spending five months visiting the Somersets and catching up on new medical advances. Then the British Colonial Office announced a new posting for her. It was one of the strangest postings on record.

Dr. Barry had spent forty-four years in service. With the exception of her first brief assignment in Plymouth, her entire career had been spent in the warm climates of tropical and subtropical posts. According to official army records, Barry was now sixty-two years of age, with only a few more years of service before retirement. In fact, she was closer to seventy.

She might logically have expected an easy posting in another warm climate. It was the customary end-of-service rotation that usually ended a long career. But despite her age and experience with tropical medicine, on November 14, 1857, the director-general of the army medical department, A. Smith, sent Barry to Canada to relieve Inspector General of Hospitals T. Alexander, who had been transferred to Malta.

Barry left England late in the year and made a stormy crossing of the Atlantic. Her ship sailed up the St. Lawrence to the port city of Montreal in Lower Canada. From there she made her way to Upper Canada and the military post of Bytown (now Ottawa), arriving early in December 1857 in the midst of a winter colder than anything she had ever imagined.

Accustomed to warmer climates, Psyche shivered with the cold and yipped indignantly. "Luckily I'm not superstitious," Barry laughed, wrapping a shawl around the little dog. "You're just feeling the cold. You'll get used to it."

"Here, you look after her," she said, handing Psyche to her servant, John. Like Barry he was accustomed to the tropics, and privately he wondered if anyone could grow accustomed to such bitter weather.

She left them outside while she hurried into the administration office, anxious to settle into her quarters and look around this strange new posting.

Chapter Ten

CANADA

BARRY LOVED CANADA. The wide-open feel of the country, the rolling sweep of the hills and the sombre tone of
evergreen trees were completely different from what she had
been used to. But the biggest change was the weather. Not
even in her student days in Scotland had she been so cold!
Gratefully she snuggled into the heavy winter gear issued by
the military. The padding she normally wore under her uniform would never be noticed here.

She settled quickly into her new quarters and then, as
inspector general of hospitals in Upper and Lower Canada,
toured the various posts that were now her responsibility. She
was not happy with what she found.

Once again she found soldiers living in appalling conditions. One look at the water supply system and storm warn-
ings flew. "This is disgraceful," she raged.

She didn't know who was more to blame. Even the least
experienced soldier should know better than to put up with
the conditions she found in some garrisons. And it was hard
to believe the officers would allow things to become so bad.
Once again her favourite threat rolled through the air: "I
should cut off their ears. All of them!"

When Barry stormed in to see the commanding officer,
she was in fine fettle. With her usual lack of tact she spelled
out in bitter detail the appalling conditions she had found.
The men might as well be drinking directly from cesspools,

she told him. There was no excuse whatever for these conditions.

Barry drew up a list of rules that the commanding officer endorsed and issued for posting. They were not difficult rules, and there were only two of them:

Obtain all drinking water upstream from the latrines and slop pools.

Dig channels so drainage water doesn't stand in stagnant pools, breeding mosquitoes and spreading disease.

The garrisons were not alone in their sewage and sanitation problems. While Barry was busy dealing with problems in the army camps of Upper Canada, civilian doctors and politicians in Toronto were trying to decide what to do about stagnant water that collected along The Esplanade, between Yonge and Church streets.

Newspapers reported that a "low form of fever" already existed. Unless the situation was corrected, "the most serious consequences" would follow. Typhus was common and deadly. City officials feared a major outbreak of either typhus or cholera, but hesitated to use the words in case they caused panic among the city's residents.

These were the same diseases Barry faced, but while she could order soldiers to make changes—on threat of serious penalties—civic officials hesitated to go that far with a civilian population. The freezing winter temperatures provided a temporary solution to Toronto's problem, but it would return in the springtime when the ice and snow melted. Barry was not willing to wait. She set out strict rules and regulations for garrison sanitation. The rules were put in place immediately and followed without question.

Then she attacked conditions inside the barracks.

"Look at this," she muttered, as she stalked from one barrack to another. "Soldiers, wives and children all in one large dormitory." Married couples had no privacy. Their beds stood in rows along with those of the other soldiers. "Women and children should not sleep in a room full of men," she told her aide, who trailed behind her taking notes. The men were coarse and crude—and too often they were drunk. Once again she presented the commanding officer with a list of complaints. He agreed completely and issued orders providing for the construction of separate rooms for married couples and their children.

Privately the commander must have wondered about this new doctor. Was no detail of the soldiers' lives to be left unexamined? As he would learn, Barry paid close attention to everything that affected the soldiers' health—even down to something that seemed as trivial as the type of fuel used for the garrison's cookstove and the heaters that warmed the soldiers' quarters.

In previous years heating and cooking consumed sixty cords of wood. It cost eleven pounds, six shillings and ten pence to hire civilian contractors to pile, saw, split and stack the fuel. To reduce expenses the army decided to switch from wood to coal. Barry opposed the move.

"I have found that wood is a much healthier fuel than coal," she explained. She might not know the names of the gases, but she knew improperly burned coal could produce fumes that were fatal. There were other dangers as well. Stored coal gave off invisible gases that caused fevers and diseases of the lungs and throat.

The quartermasters raised their eyebrows and allowed themselves a good laugh at the notion of invisible gases. Surely she was exaggerating!

Barry turned to her favourite weapon—a quill pen—and prepared to do battle. She wrote a memo to the military secretary.

I feel it my bounden duty to observe that during long services in various parts of the World, I have invariably found Wood as fuel for the use of Troops much more healthy than Coals inasmuch as the gas which emanates from the Coals when amalgamated with the atmosphere . . . becomes exceedingly deleterious in generating fevers of the typhoid type and diseases of the respiratory organs. . . . Even when covered, [coals] render exceedingly unhealthy the surrounding atmosphere.

In the Island of Corfu, Fever of a Malignant kind occurred in the Officers Quarters and Artillery Barracks in the Citadel, which was discovered to be owing to Coals accumulated by the Contractor . . . immediately under the Walls of the Citadel.

At my recommendation, in which I was joined with that of Col. Hall of the Royal Engineers, The Coals were removed, the Citadel became healthy and there was no recurrence of the disease.

There was strong opposition. Coal was cheaper than wood, and as always the military was anxious to cut costs. But Barry refused to give up. Eventually she managed to convince the authorities that the men's health was worth more than the few pennies that would be saved by the proposed change. So compelling were her arguments that even though the price of wood went up (the 1858 bill for sawing, splitting, piling and re-piling sixty and one-half cords of wood came to twelve pounds and two shillings) the army continued to use it.

One of Barry's ongoing concerns was food. After forty years in the tropics, where a wide range of fruits and vegetables was available year round, the Canadian menu was bleak. She still remembered her first taste of coconut jelly, that smooth sweet inner lining of young coconuts that was such a delight to eat and so different from the tough, firm white chunks that lined mature coconuts. There was no way to transport any of her favourite tropical foods, and she missed them dreadfully—the tongue-tingling flavour of mangoes, bursting with juice, plucked fresh from the tree; the creamy sweetness of little pink "ladyfinger" bananas or the crisp fried slabs of plantain banana; the astringent taste of star apples, whose waxy wings became almost transparent as the fruit ripened.

For a vegetarian the Canadian menu was especially limited. "I think if I see one more turnip I shall die," she complained to Psyche, poking at a platter of boiled turnip, boiled potato and heavy bread. "Don't the cooks know how to do anything but boil food?"

The menu for soldiers was not much better. Boiled beef and bread was the basic diet. "It's traditional, but it isn't healthy," she told the quartermaster, who was responsible for purchasing provisions. "The markets are full of pumpkin. Why not serve it along with the bread and beef?"

In the 1850s pumpkin was a staple winter food in many Canadian homes. Sliced and dried, it stored well and was used as a vegetable during the long days of winter.

"The men won't eat it," he said flatly.

"We'll see about that!" she replied.

He was right. The pumpkin was largely ignored and left on the plates to be mixed into swill for the pigs.

In spring and summer local residents gathered greens from the nearby forests to supplement their diets and add variety. Barry sent her servant, John, out into the woods to gather greens for her.

"Why not have the soldiers do the same thing?" she suggested to the commanding officer. When men were sent out to pick greens, they grumbled and complained. The job of a soldier was not picking leaves! They came back with scant handfuls.

Barry was furious. "Surely they can't be so dense that they prefer to suffer from scurvy, pellagra and other diseases rather than do something as unmanly as gathering greens." If they would not gather their own greens, she would find some other way to supplement their diets.

She ordered the quartermaster to buy vegetables and greens from the local markets.

"They won't eat them," he grumbled. "That's not fit food for a man."

"Nonsense," Barry snapped.

They wouldn't. The pig swill contained platters of costly greens.

She worried continually about the steady diet of boiled beef, but little else was available. Then she discovered Lake Ontario whitefish. It was a local favourite whose fame spread to other areas as well. Lake fishermen shipped hundreds of pounds of whitefish to markets throughout the area. The huge fish grew from six to eight feet in length.

Confidently Barry ordered the cooks to prepare whitefish, sturgeon and other types of fish for the men.

"No use," they said. "The men won't eat it."

"Of course they will!" she retorted.

They wouldn't. The soldiers rebelled. They refused to eat the fish. They wanted their boiled beef.

Barry shook her head in defeat.

"All right," she told the quartermaster. "Give them boiled beef, but at least include salt pork and mutton on the menu so they aren't eating the same thing day after day."

"Can't do it," the quartermaster told her. Supplies had to be tendered. There was no tender for salt pork or fresh mutton.

Barry couldn't force the men to eat healthier meals, and her efforts on their behalf didn't always succeed, but she never stopped trying. Despite her concern for them, she was not popular with the troops. It was easy to understand why. As she grew older she had become more direct in her comments. During sick parades she had the habit of walking along the lines of troopers, muttering as she went, "Filthy beasts. Filthy beasts. Go wash yourselves." It was probably good advice but could have been given in a more kindly manner.

During her first winter in Canada, Barry bought a sleigh

and several lap robes of shaggy buffalo hides to keep her warm as she made her rounds. With Psyche snuggled under the robes, she rode in her sleigh through the streets and byways of Ottawa and the surrounding area. The jingling of sleigh bells on passing vehicles was like a musical background that added to her enjoyment. In springtime a horse and buggy allowed her to travel easily in the rural areas surrounding the army posts.

In March she had her first encounter with maple syrup when maple taffy was served in the officers' mess. "What's this?" she asked, cutting off a small piece of the flat sweet slab served on a platter of snow.

"It's sugaring-off season," a mess-mate explained, "which means the sap is running. They make this from the maple trees."

Warily Barry looked at him. Surely he was making a joke at her expense. During her time in the tropics she had visited many sugar cane plantations and watched with interest as the coarse canes were ground up to yield the thick sweet syrup that was converted into molasses, syrup, table sugar and rum. But she had never heard of syrup taken from a tree.

Barry's table companions watched with expectant grins as she took her first taste of the treat. "Why, this is wonderful!" Eagerly she reached towards the platter for a larger piece.

Later she visited a sugar farm and watched the process with interest, tasting the syrup as it dripped through wooden spigots into buckets hung from the trees, looking on as the farmer boiled down the sap and converted it to maple syrup, maple sugar or the maple taffy that was a favourite with young and old.

In the 1850s farmers produced over five million pounds of maple syrup and sugar every year. But unlike sugar cane, their product was not used to make rum or other liquors, which, according to Barry, was just as well. Barry was outraged by the number of drunken men she saw in the streets. They appeared to be everywhere. Gin merchants were attracted to military posts, soldiers spent much of their pay on liquor and beer, and civilians seemed to drink just as much as the soldiers.

Drink, however, was part of the daily routine in early Canada. Whiskey and other alcoholic beverages were served at work bees, weddings, auction sales, funerals and even revival camp meetings. With a population of only thirty thousand people, Toronto supported 152 taverns and 206 beer shops. There was easy access to alcohol in almost every city, town, village and hamlet in Upper and Lower Canada. Barry, of course, was unsuccessful in her attempts to reduce the amount of alcohol consumed by the soldiers. But she redoubled her efforts to protect their health.

She prescribed regular doses of cod liver oil for every soldier in the garrison, ordering between thirty and fifty gallons of the mixture each year and ensuring that every soldier in the camp lined up to take his doses. It was not a popular move.

When Barry arrived in Canada, it had been forty-five years since she graduated from the University of Edinburgh. During those years, she had studied and remained up to date on new procedures, surgical discoveries and inventions. Her supply order for the month of March 1859 included many items not yet on the general medical form, such as the urinometer, an instrument used to determine the specific gravity of urine and useful in diagnosis. She asked for special equipment to regulate and standardize doses of medicine, such as graduated specula and a hydrometer to measure the strength of spirits used in filling prescriptions and making medicines. New medicines were listed on her orders as well. She read the medical journals carefully and ordered new compounds such as chloroform, ergot and others as they became available.

Barry was most grateful for chloroform, which rendered her patients unconscious during surgery. Now speed was no longer paramount, and there was ample time for the precise work required by more intricate surgeries.

During peacetime, however, surgery played only a small role in army medicine. The surgeon generally reverted to the role of general practitioner. So it was with Barry, but she found much to keep her busy.

Barry didn't spend all her hours working, however. As always she was interested in learning more about local medical practices. In the tropics she had tried to uncover the secrets of local herbal doctors, witch doctors, voodoo doctors and shamans. Patiently she had dried and mixed batches of leaves, barks, herbs and other ingredients, recording her findings in the search for elixirs and cures. In Canada she had little opportunity to learn about native medicines and healing customs, but she did question local healing women about the herbs they used.

Wherever she was, Barry enjoyed watching sporting events. In South Africa she had shared with Lord Charles a love of fine horses and an appreciation for horse racing. She was an indifferent rider herself but found great pleasure in watching horse races, polo and gymkhanas.

In Canada she found the familiar sports played everywhere in the British Empire—rugby, soccer and cricket—but she also encountered sports she had never seen before. Snowshoe races and dogsled races were great fun to watch. She drove her sleigh to the riverbanks, where she could watch speeding toboggans carry passengers screaming with delight or see skaters in graceful flight along the frozen surface of the water. Wrapped warmly in her buffalo robes, she murmured to Psyche, "If I were younger I think I'd like to try that."

Another event she enjoyed watching was a new game popular with both the troops and the local residents. It was called curling and seemed to require the combined skills of lawn bowling, boccie and shuffleboard.

If Barry did not take an active part in sporting events, she did enjoy the social events that crowded everyone's calendar. All year, people enjoyed going to dances, playing cards and attending dinner parties that lasted until the small hours of the morning. It was an age when conversation was a major form of entertainment, and Barry was a brilliant conversationalist. She had a sharp sense of humour, a quick wit and a wealth of stories about her time in the colonies.

She wasn't above adding to a good story either, and some of her tales were completely fictional. She told fascinated listeners stories about her broken engagements, the loss of all her family papers and jewels in a shipwreck and other spectacular events that may or may not have happened.

Barry found much to enjoy in the Canadas. In Toronto she could join a group of officers at the new pleasure resort called, simply, the Island. Minstrel shows, comic and sentimental singing, and dramatic performances were featured. Other diversions included stage plays at the Royal Lyceum Theatre, where famous actors from Europe and the United States recreated everything from broad farces and drawing-room comedies to the classical works of Shakespeare and the Greek tragedies.

When her duties took her to Montreal, she enjoyed watching ships leave and enter the city's busy port. In the 1850s more than 170 sailing ships visited Montreal each year. Only a handful of steamers used the harbour, but they controlled most of the busy canal traffic. Canal steamers were small narrow boats called puffers. A recently invented screw propeller powered the boats. At first, passengers were nervous about the noisy little puffers and preferred to ride on barges towed behind them. This system reminded them of the horse-drawn canal boats they had known in Europe.

Puffers and steamers were unattractive, but as they scuttled around the beautiful tall-masted sailing ships, it became obvious that they were more manoeuvrable, dependable and efficient. Later, as travellers became more accustomed to puffers, they were enlarged to carry more passengers.

A few years before Barry arrived in Canada, the first *Maid of the Mist* was launched below Niagara Falls. A ride in the little boat was the highlight of a visit to the falls, and Barry joined other officers visiting the falls to pass by the curtain of water. "Niagara comes from a native word meaning 'Thundering Waters,'" the guide shouted, trying to make himself heard above the roaring downpour. "It certainly suits." Visitors could only agree.

New times and new technologies were sweeping across the two Canadas as in the rest of the world. One of the most exciting events involved the telegraph cable, soon to be laid under the Atlantic Ocean to connect Ireland with Newfoundland. Two ships, the *Agamemnon* and the *Niagara*, carried and released the fifteen hundred miles of cable onto the ocean floor. Soon news from Britain and Europe could cross the Atlantic in seconds.

Other exciting events kept the colony buzzing. During the winter of 1857–1858, attention focused on the question of unity between Upper and Lower Canada. Newspapers carried stories and editorials both for and against the move. When an election was called, candidates also took a stand on the question. Barry's British citizenship gave her the right to vote in these elections, which increased her interest in the question.

Some writers and politicians looked beyond the immediate issue of uniting the colonies. An editorial in one newspaper said, "The one great question of Upper Canada, standing out above all others in importance, is Representation by Population. Until this is granted, it is useless to talk about national harmony or to expect the union to work satisfactorily."

When the votes were counted, one of the successful candidates was a young man who won the right to represent

Kingston. His name was John A. Macdonald. In later years he became the first prime minister of the Dominion of Canada.

Barry enjoyed listening to political debates on the issues of the day. She was no stranger to politics. Even within the medical profession she had seen examples of political influence at work. For many years, and in many places, Barry had lobbied for control of medical practices. It was a matter of concern to many doctors. In January 1858 a committee of doctors called a special meeting to consider forming a central board of examiners to examine all candidates for licences to practise medicine.

"It should have been done long ago," she agreed.

Local doctors argued about how long students needed to study to qualify as doctors. Some practised after only two years of study. Others studied up to four years to complete their qualifications. A few, like Barry, continued well beyond the basics.

One group of doctors said that *what* students learned was more important than how long they studied. A Dr. Rolph, who ran a medical school in Upper Canada, said the young men in his establishment studied only three months but were as proficient as many of those who had studied four years in Europe or England.

"What utter rot!" Barry fumed. "I hope he gets seriously ill and needs the services of a doctor or a surgeon. Then we'll see how he feels about someone who has studied for only three months!"

During her years of service she had met a good number of doctors, both military and civilian. Some were very talented. Others should never have been allowed near a patient. It was high time a method was put in place to weed out the incompetents. "When will they realize that if they want good medicine, they have to set high standards?" Barry mused. She knew the committee had to move carefully, but surely they could set standards in place a little more quickly. To her, always impatient for improvements, they seemed to move like snails.

After much discussion the committee agreed that an examination was the fairest way to decide who was ready to practise. The committee also suggested setting standards for anyone who wanted to practise medicine in Canada but had trained elsewhere. Five doctors, including one named Bethune, drafted the final petition to be sent to the government.

The long winter nights gradually shortened. Buds began to swell on the trees, and ice loosened its grip on the rivers. One Tuesday afternoon, early in April 1858, Barry heard a commotion outside her quarters and recognized the voices of some fellow officers.

"We're going down to Allanburgh to watch them fill the Welland Canal. If you don't want to miss it, you'd better hurry."

The Welland Canal was a major feat of engineering, linking Fort Erie to Lake Ontario. It was just one expression of the rapid industrial expansion taking place everywhere. Now, too, an element of nationalism arose. Canadian currency was about to change from the British pounds, shillings and pence to decimal coinage like that of Canada's neighbour, the United States of America. It was not a unanimously popular move, and many residents feared the confusion that would result when the new system became official. The newly minted coinage included tiny five- and ten-cent silver pieces and bronze pennies, which were larger than today's quarters.

Among Barry's more arduous responsibilities were the tours of inspection throughout Upper and Lower Canada. One such trip began on June 30, 1858. Barry travelled by train and horse-drawn carriage to Lower Canada for a two-day visit, back to Kingston in Upper Canada from July 12–15, Toronto from July 15–17, Niagara from July 17–19, Toronto again from July 19–20, Kingston again from July 20–22 and back to Ottawa on July 23. It was a gruelling trip. Barry and Psyche bounced uncomfortably around in the carriage as it swayed between ruts and lurched from one pothole to the next.

"Why are the roads in such poor condition?" she asked her driver. It had never been a problem in the tropics, although there the heavy rain of the monsoons often washed the roads away.

"It's the frost," he explained. "The winter cold causes the road surfaces to buckle and bend."

In late September, Barry watched in fascination as the colours of a Canadian autumn spread across the country: glowing red maples, golden tamaracks, yellow birches and stands of evergreens intermingled like the colours on an artist's palette. Surely, she thought, her Uncle James, the painter, had never seen anything more beautiful than this.

The beauty of the scenery, however, did nothing to appease her anger when she discovered her authority had been bypassed in the matter of purchasing food for hospital patients, a subject which naturally led her back to her ongoing complaints about food served to the troopers.

All through September, October and November, packets of letters flew back and forth between Barry's office and the office of the military secretary at Montreal. By the end of December she was still flooding them with memorandums and letters, challenging the actions of everyone connected with the affair and going so far as to provide a cost analysis, based on a market survey, to prove that her position was not only correct but would be financially superior to the contracts undertaken by the government.

While both sides considered the next step in this particular battle, Barry continued her regular work. Early in the spring of 1859, an epidemic of influenza swept the country.

Barry, who had been plagued by repeated bouts of bronchitis, fell ill. She prescribed her own medication and tried to cure herself, but nothing worked. She became sicker and sicker until at last friends called a doctor in to examine her.

Although Barry had made a lifetime habit of flooding sickrooms with fresh air and sunshine, she insisted on closing the windows and drawing the curtains in her own room. Then she turned the lamps to their lowest settings before allowing the young Canadian doctor, G.W. Campbell, to enter her room.

Campbell, not long out of medical school, suggested more light would be helpful. Barry replied that there was enough light and suggested he simply get on with his examination. She kept her bedcovers pulled up and tucked tightly under her chin, and while the young doctor attempted to make a diagnosis, she proceeded to tell him precisely what was wrong with her without allowing him to verify her condition for himself.

It was a difficult situation for Campbell. This was a very senior doctor and a very testy patient. He did not want to antagonize her needlessly. He agreed she had influenza and prescribed medication and bed rest to help her recover.

In later years, when Campbell became dean of medicine at McGill University, he used the story as an example for his students, telling them he missed out on the most interesting patient examination of his career. "I was intimidated by the rank and experience of my patient," he told his students. He smiled and then urged them never to make the same mistake. The message was clear. No matter who they examined, they should not take anyone's word for what the patient's condition was—least of all the word of the patient! In Barry's case, of course, the examination would have made no difference to the diagnosis or the treatment. She did have influenza, and what Campbell had prescribed was perfectly correct. But he often wondered what would have happened had he been allowed to make his own examination.

Gradually Barry recovered, but she did not return to her original good health. Although no one else knew it, she was almost seventy years old and people her age do not recover as quickly as younger patients. Always impatient, Barry spent a short time resting and then declared herself ready to return to work.

Her colleagues and associates did not feel she was strong enough to resume her duties, and on April 7, 1859, she received a letter from the Home Office directing her to return to England for the purpose of being examined by the board of medical officers. She was sent to England on sick leave and spent a few weeks in London resting and regaining her strength before facing the board. After a brief examination they pronounced her unfit for active duty.

On July 19, 1859, she was placed on half pay—the military phrase for retirement. Barry protested but to no avail. On September 26, 1859, her replacement was named. Dr. G. Taylor was now principal medical officer in Upper and Lower Canada.

Barry lived quietly in England for almost six years with Psyche and her servant, John. She returned to the West Indies for at least one visit, but for the most part she stayed in London.

She could have told an intriguing story about her career, but she chose to keep her secrets. Unlike so many of her colleagues she did not write her memoirs. She kept no diary, journal or even her personal letters. She left no discussion of medical advances, no commentary on the techniques she used, despite their proven superiority, no record of the truly unique cases she attended, not the least of which was the Munnik Caesarean.

She must have smiled to herself each day as she left her

lodgings to take Psyche for a walk. As she passed the post on the street corner, she could see the name she had given up half a century earlier. Dr. James Barry's final home was 14 Margaret Street, Cavendish Square, London.

When she died on July 15, 1865, the woman who prepared her body for burial discovered the secret of her gender, but there seemed to be little more than mild curiosity about her finding. No official action was taken. There was a small flurry of letters to *The Lancet,* the leading medical journal, from doctors who had known Barry.

On May 18, 1867, some two years after her death, a young journalist published an account of Barry's life and death under the title *A Mystery Still.* Charles Dickens was at that time a journalist who earned his living writing for newspapers. He reported that Barry was "a gentleman every inch of him," although in Dickens' own words, "this is not literally saying very much for him, seeing he was but a little man." Dickens reported that Barry had a fair allowance from some source or other but that he never spoke of any relatives or friends outside of the military profession. Throughout the article, Dickens praised Barry's medical skills but laughed at his mannerisms and appearance. In Dickens' words, "frail in body, unique in appearance and eccentric in manner, [Barry] ensured respect by his capacity, and as he could be courteous when he pleased, his oddities were excused by his colleagues."

In her later years, Barry had mellowed, and Dickens reported that during the doctor's time in Jamestown on St. Helena, those who knew him asserted that "selfish, odd and cranky as he was, he had kindness for the poor and was charitable without ostentation."

Dickens' comments appear to be based on interviews with those who knew Barry from various postings. And while Barry may have mellowed personally, according to Dickens' informants, she continued to be an administrative terror.

Dickens notes, "His presence at the hospital was a signal for the juniors to be all on the alert. The soldiers liked him and trusted his skill, but woe betide the laggard medico who was not there to receive the PMO [Principal Medical Officer] or who had swerved one hair's-breadth from his instructions." Barry's friends of former days held by her to the last. "He was often ailing and the kind ladies of his Cape patron's family [the Somersets] would take him out driving in the park, and would have him to dinner," Dickens reported.

Barry hoped to be honoured with a knighthood for her service and had ordered a new uniform for the occasion. Before this could happen, however, she became ill and took to her bed, shivering and feverish. She died soon after.

Dr. James Barry was buried at Kensal Green late in July 1865. The grave is registered under the name she used from the time she entered Edinburgh University until her death. There was no autopsy because there was no *official* reason to doubt that Barry was exactly who she said she was: a man born in 1795. On military records, that is how she remains.

Epilogue

Given the stunning revelation of Barry's gender, the question often asked is why there was no autopsy. The official response was that there was no need. Barry had been seriously ill with chronic bronchitis, residual weakness from attacks of cholera and yellow fever, and had reached what was in those times an advanced age. Her death was not unusual; that is, there were no suspicious circumstances surrounding it that would have justified an autopsy. There was no suspicion of foul play or medical misadventure. Nor was there any doubt about her identity. Her physician was not concerned with her sex but rather with certifying that a patient who was personally known to him had died of a known illness. From an official point of view, there were no inconsistencies in the case.

Questions about Barry's sex arose after her death, but there was no reason to exhume her body to complete an autopsy. To officials her sex had no bearing on the question of her death. To pursue the case further would only have been to satisfy curiosity, and curiosity is not sufficient grounds for such a drastic procedure with all its legal and religious implications.

Barry's career as a doctor was recorded by Isobel Rae in her 1958 book *The Strange Case of Dr. James Barry*. But the question of Barry's real identity had never been answered conclusively. My research had to begin before those well-documented years. How, then, at this late date could one trace Dr. James Barry back to her roots as the young Irish girl Margaret Anne Bulkley?

At one time I had the good fortune to work for several years with then Sergeant Fred Bodnaruk, of the Royal Canadian Mounted Police. Bodnaruk was, and is, a highly respected investigator, noted in the force for unraveling several especially puzzling cases. At one point I asked how he began his investigations and how he sorted fact from fiction when analyzing alibis. The best lies, he said, were those which contained the most truth. These were the hardest to shake. But if you could find the one weak link, the whole story would often unravel.

The search for James Barry's identity had to begin with what was true. More than one hundred years after her death, there were no remaining witnesses. But Bodnaruk had given me one other clue, and it became the first peg on which to hang my investigation.

People assuming new identities often retain some tie to their past through their name. They might choose their mother's maiden name or the name of some other relative. Often they choose a name with the same initials as their former name. James Barry, the artist, and James Barry, the doctor, had been linked by the doctor's own words. She made reference several times to her Uncle James Barry. Some earlier accounts of the mysterious doctor's story had suggested that the artist might have fathered an illegitimate child who became Dr. Barry.

Fortunately there is a good deal of well-documented information about the artist James Barry, who was a member of the Royal Academy of Art. He was the first to endure my scrutiny. The artist lived in London as did Dr. Barry. Or at least Dr. Barry *said* she was from London. But biographies of the artist revealed that although he lived in England, he was in fact Irish, born in Cork. It appeared that the artist had no connection with the doctor after all. But in one biography there is a single line stating that after the death of James Barry, the painter, his estate was handled by his sister, a Mrs. Bulkley.

Dr. Barry's housekeeper was named Mrs. Bulkley. Was this just coincidence? Perhaps not. At times Barry had referred to her as "my aunt, Mrs. Bulkley." Could an aunt be a housekeeper? Of course. But if she was an aunt, how precisely was she related? She could have been the sister of either Barry's mother or her father.

Mrs. Jo Currie, a librarian in the University of Edinburgh Archives, told me she believed Dr. Barry was not from London, as her papers indicated, but from Ireland. It was an interesting comment. Perhaps there *was* a connection between the two James Barrys. Gradually other information reinforced this notion. Pictures of James Barry RA and James Barry MD showed a family resemblance. There appeared to be a strong possibility that they were related—not as illegitimate child and careless father, but in a perfectly reputable relationship as uncle and niece—and that Mary Anne Bulkley was not an aunt but Dr. Barry's mother and a sister to the artist.

The links grew stronger and stronger. The Earl of Buchan and General Miranda, the men to whom Dr. Barry dedicated her graduation thesis, were loyal friends of the artist and continued that loyalty to his sister and niece.

A box of Buchan family papers discovered in the Walpole Library in Connecticut held copies of letters from Mary Anne Bulkley to the earl regarding the disposition of Barry's paintings and other matters. Other scraps of information appeared. The Venezuelan National Library contains a letter written in 1810 from James Barry, then a student at the University of Edinburgh, to General Miranda. Barry mentions dining with the Earl of Buchan and of telling Buchan of

Miranda's generosity in allowing Barry to make use of the general's wonderful library. In this letter, Barry refers to herself as "Barry's nephew"—another reference to the artist James Barry. There is an enigmatic line at the end of the letter, referring to Mrs. Bulkley's daughter as a "cousin."

As far as can be discovered, Margaret Bulkley had no cousins. Could the reference have been to Margaret herself? Was this perhaps a device to explain a reference Mrs. Bulkley may have made to her daughter?

In a letter dated October 15, 1811, Buchan asks a favour of Dr. Robert Anderson, requesting that Anderson and Dr. Irving "look at the Latinity of His [Barry's] thesis," then adding, "He means to go by invitation of General Miranda to The Caracas."

This confirmed my hunch that Barry had never intended to practise medicine in England, but from the first planned to use her skills in Venezuela under the patronage and protection of General Miranda. Her disguise was likely seen only as a temporary measure to see her through medical school, which was closed to her as a woman. Circumstances forced her to continue it for the remainder of her life.

My search took me to Cork, the family home of John Barry and his wife, the former Juliana Reardon, parents to both James Barry, the artist, and Mary Anne Bulkley, the doctor's mother. I walked along Water Lane, visited the Blackpool suburb, crossed the bridges of the River Lee and located Barry's pub. It was an exciting time.

The next stop was Dublin and the home of Ireland's national archives. There the search abruptly hit a dead end. A 1925 fire in Dublin's Four Courts, the site of the archives, destroyed almost seventy-five percent of all records. There were no duplicates, no microfiches or computer disks to back up the information. The loss has dead-ended many investigations, and it appeared this one, too, would fall by the wayside.

But re-examining information that was available, I was drawn again to the Walpole Library papers. There I learned that Margaret wrote most of the letters signed by Mary Anne. This offered the first possibility of proving that Margaret Anne Bulkley and James Barry were the same person. Forensic graphology might give conclusive evidence one way or another.

A copy of a letter known to be written by Margaret and a copy of a report written by Dr. James Barry, obtained from the National Archives in Canada, were given to William D. (Tex) Thorpe, who agreed to examine the documents. Thorpe has a long history of forensic document examination and is an expert witness at the Court of Queen's Bench in Canada and the Superior Court in Washington State. His skills are unquestioned.

When he compared the two sets of documents, it was his opinion that the same hand had written both samples. Barry's true identity was at long last given the most empirical confirmation it had received to date.

It is tantalizing to think that somewhere in a dusty trunk tucked away in an attic there might yet be a packet of Barry's personal letters or a diary providing further information about this enigmatic personality. Regardless of the facts and fictions presented here, Dr. James Barry lived an extraordinary life during one of the most turbulent and revolutionary periods in recent history. If she did so disguised as a man, as I believe she did, her story is all the more remarkable.